It couldn't be him, it couldn't!

If it was him, why didn't he say something? He must have recognised her in return. For she knew it was no ghost that stood beside her chair, but a solid man, one she'd known only too well.

'I'm Nick Coleman, the new medical director of the company. I didn't catch your name, I'm afraid.'

'Rose—Rose Maslen.' Holding her breath, Rose waited for some comment, some flicker of recognition. But his expression didn't change.

Dear Reader

Christine Adams's second book, LOVE BLOOMS, shows how the air ambulance service works, and looks at amnesia. Elisabeth Scott's story, set in general practice in the north of England, has Neil's expertise clashing with Sarah's local knowledge. Laura MacDonald looks at trying to go back when people have grown away from each other, and Margaret Barker's Scottish general practice story shows how Ian's understanding helps Heather to cope with her past. We hope you like them.

The Editor

Christine Adams is a registered nurse living in the West Country, who has worked for many years in the National Health Service and still nurses part-time. She has been writing for the past ten years, mainly short stories and articles. She finds the dramas and tensions in the medical world an ideal background in which to find plots and storylines.

Recent titles by the same author:

DEMPSEY'S DILEMMA

LOVE BLOOMS

BY
CHRISTINE ADAMS

*To Dear Janet
Love from
Christine Adams
(Edna Trewella)*

MILLS & BOON LIMITED
ETON HOUSE   18–24 PARADISE ROAD
RICHMOND   SURREY   TW9 1SR

All the characters in this book have no existence outside the imagination of the Author, and have no relation whatsoever to anyone bearing the same name or names. They are not even distantly inspired by any individual known or unknown to the Author, and all the incidents are pure invention.

All Rights Reserved. The text of this publication or any part thereof may not be reproduced or transmitted in any form or by any means, electronic or mechanical, including photocopying, recording, storage in an information retrieval system, or otherwise, without the written permission of the publisher.

This book is sold subject to the condition that it shall not, by way of trade or otherwise, be lent, resold, hired out or otherwise circulated without the prior consent of the publisher in any form of binding or cover other than that in which it is published and without a similar condition including this condition being imposed on the subsequent purchaser.

First published in Great Britain 1993 by Mills & Boon Limited

© Christine Adams 1993

*Australian copyright 1993
Philippine copyright 1993
This edition 1993*

ISBN 0 263 78092 9

*Set in 10½ on 12 pt Linotron Times
03-9304-49346*

*Typeset in Great Britain by Centracet, Cambridge
Made and printed in Great Britain*

PROLOGUE

THE whole landscape was the colour of sand, the shadows of the rocky outcrops and a few scrubby bushes the only variation in a never-ending sludgy grey landscape that reached to the horizon.

The girl licked her lips, wincing as the layer of grit that clung to her mouth scratched drily against her tongue. She frowned, sliding a finger around the inside of the neck of her nurse's tunic; the thin cotton material felt as heavy as the thickest tweed as it clung to her skin. Dazzled by the glare of the African sun despite her large dark glasses, at first she didn't see the extra swirl of powdery sand. It touched the edge of the runway, then the whine of an engine percolated through her fatigue and she stared at the approaching lorry. It drew up beside the dusty air ambulance parked on the narrow strip of concrete. The dust raised by the lorry's wheels reached the sandstone building to her left, which was visible only because of the stark black shadow of its doorway.

Nervously straightening the waistband of her navy trousers, she moved towards the vehicle, the sudden silence as the engine cut almost painful to her ears. Swiftly her clear grey eyes swept across the group of men standing upright in the rear of the truck, white robes a sharp contrast to the dark unsmiling faces.

She gasped as she realised that the protective fence post around them consisted of guns held upright.

She had been told most emphatically before her trip that she would be in no danger. But the sight in front of her wasn't very encouraging, though she hadn't time to worry just then.

A door slammed and a man dropped lightly to the ground from the driver's seat; he strolled towards her, his khaki shirt and trousers emphasising the tigerish walk, his smile a flash of white in his sun-darkened olive skin.

Was this the doctor who was supposed to be meeting her? the girl wondered, chewing anxiously at her lower lip. He was certainly nothing like any doctor she'd known before.

'Well, what have we here?' he drawled, pulling his battered bush hat further forward to cast a shadow over his face. He turned towards the men in the lorry, still standing rigidly to attention despite the rays of the sun beating down from a brassy sky. 'What an unexpected flower to find blooming in the desert! It looks as though our journey could have unlooked-for benefits.'

The girl shivered in spite of the heat and drew her head back sharply as his arrogant hand traced the line of her cheek with a surprisingly delicate touch, at variance with his aggressive masculinity, which she could almost taste. Shrugging aside his offer of help, she picked up her medical bag and climbed into the cab of the waiting truck, ignoring the look of amusement on his face as he swung up into the seat beside her.

The engine scratched, then roared into smoky life, belches of fumes pouring out from behind them, the acrid smell mixing with an incongruous drift of lemon-sharp cologne from her companion.

They saw little other traffic as they bounced along a road that was no more than a series of potholes; a red and yellow painted bus passed by, and a group of children in brightly flowered smocks that barely covered their skipping black legs waved and smiled at the lorry, ignoring the sight of the armed men at the rear.

The girl risked a glance at the driver from the corner of her eye, noticing the powerful hands resting lightly on the steering-wheel, the hawklike profile of nose and chin, deep slashes drawing attention to the line of his cheek.

'There's nothing to fear,' he murmured softly; his hand rested lightly on her knee for a moment, and she was shocked at the sensation that started through her body from the casual touch.

'I'm not afraid,' she countered sharply, resenting his physical power, then she wished she'd remained silent. For he pulled her hand towards his mouth, still steering the vehicle as skilfully as before, and gently touched her palm with his lips, folding her fingers over as though to seal the kiss in place. The tingle that spread along her arm and set every part of her aflame made her gasp, even as she snatched her hand free.

'What on earth do you think you're doing?' she snapped, her voice grating as harshly as though filled with sand from the surrounding scrubland. He didn't reply, merely smiled for a moment, then began a tuneless whistle that was just as unnerving as his unexpected caress. She smoothed the hand he had kissed, and wouldn't have been surprised to have seen an imprint left by the fire of his lips.

A crackle of thunder sounded in the distance, bringing a feel of electricity to the inside of the cab. Or was it the effect of the man beside her that made every hair seem to stand on end, that sent a tingle into every nerve end she possessed?

Perhaps she should have been warned about the risks of travelling with this man, if he had the power to disturb her senses as rapidly as this. To her jangling nerves it seemed that the dangers of passing through a countryside at war to reach her patient wouldn't be the only threat she would have to face in the next few days.

CHAPTER ONE

'HELLO, Rose Maslen speaking.' Hurriedly Rose seized the telephone receiver at its first ring, looking anxiously over her shoulder at the carrycot in the corner of the room. With a sigh of relief she saw that Timmy hadn't stirred.

'Hello, Rose, it's Alan. Can you fit in a trip tomorrow? I need a nurse escort to take two parties to Cardiology at Cosborough. They'd be going separately and are both having cardiac catheterisation, so it will take most of the day.' Alan Pollock, the director of Fleetline, a private air and road ambulance company, still spoke with a soft West Country burr, and Rose had to strain to hear him.

'What time do you want me to start?' Pulling the telephone flex to its fullest length, she sank down on to the shabby settee that took up most of the space in the living-room of her flat and sprawled along it, her long tanned legs, topped by brief peach-coloured shorts, resting inelegantly on the arm.

'About ten. You'd be able to have a break while you're waiting. I'd like someone with some cardiac experience if possible.'

'Are they both going from the same hospital?' she asked.

'Yes, and I thought it might suit you, as it's a road

trip. I know you're not too keen on air trips at present, as they take you away from Timmy.'

'Hang on a second, I'll have a quick peep at the kitchen calendar to see if Melanie is able to babysit tomorrow.'

Resting the receiver on the coffee-table, Rose darted a swift look at the sleeping baby as she passed, a smile crossing her face at the sight of his small hand like a starfish resting gently on his soft downy cheek.

A glance at the calendar showed a reassuring available note in Melanie's scrawl, and Rose returned to the telephone and wrote the details of the booking for the following day.

'Before you hang up,' Alan cut in as she started to say, 'Goodbye.' 'Don't forget the seminar on Saturday. I'd like all the staff, particularly the nurses and paramedics, to make it if they can. I've got a new syringe pump for use in the road and air ambulances and I also want to cover oxygen saturations at different altitudes again. And,' Alan paused dramatically, 'our new medical director is coming along, and it would be friendly if we have a good turn-out of staff to welcome him.'

'I'll try and get there, but of course I can't make any promises,' she told him. 'What's the new director called?'

'Sorry, got to go—the other phone's ringing and I'm the only one in the office at the moment. We'll pick you up at ten tomorrow, all right?'

'OK,' Rose said drily, staring down at the receiver in her hand.

'I'm going to be busy, Timmy,' she murmured, writing her notes more legibly, 'and, much as I hate to leave you yet again, Alan seems anxious that I get there on Saturday. I wonder what Melanie's doing?'

A welcoming smell of chicken casserole greeted her as she went into the kitchen and replaced the calendar on the hook, before picking up the kettle and filling it. Plugging it in, Rose perched on the edge of the bright yellow kitchen stool and gazed out through the narrow window on to her tiny patch of garden, where, despite the poor soil, she'd managed to encourage a fuchsia to grow. Its ballerina-like blossoms now danced a hurried fling in the breeze that drifted softly towards the back of the house.

Still lost in thought, Rose made herself a pot of tea, buttered a fruit bun and returned to the sitting-room, placing the tray on the table beside the settee.

A small sound from the carrycot drew her attention but then, as all was quiet again, she sat down, poured herself a cup of tea and stirred in a defiant spoonful of sugar before sipping it slowly.

It wasn't going to be long before she'd have to think about alternative arrangements for Timmy's care. The sight of the date as she'd looked at the calendar just now had brought it home to her that Melanie would soon finish her course and would be moving back to the Midlands.

'And that'll be just you and me then, Timmy, and where am I going to find someone as good as

Melanie to take care of a three-month-old baby while I'm working?' Rose sighed to her sleeping son.

But she hadn't time to worry just now, for there was her uniform to press for the following day, supper to prepare for Melanie and herself, then her favourite part of the day, Timmy's feed and bath.

Drinking the last of the tea, Rose took the tray through to the kitchen, washed her cup and saucer, then dropped new potatoes into the bowl, before scraping off their paper-fine skins.

The soft June evening was full of golden light, the heat of the earlier part of the day softened to a pleasant warmth; it was quiet, with just the dull roar of traffic from the motorway in the background, and the noise of an occasional jet coming in to land at Gatwick.

A swarm of gnats appeared from the trees across the road, with an accompanying squadron of wheeling swifts that dotted the skyline like black arrows. Rose rested her arms on the edge of the sink, her clear grey eyes staring thoughtfully. She'd been lucky to get this flat, but on a warm evening such as this she had to admit to feeling stifled, especially when she thought back to the large garden at her father's house.

'No use moping, Rose, my girl,' she told herself briskly. 'With Dad trailing all round the world, those happy childhood days aren't coming back.' She felt a familiar pang go through her. It was sad that history was repeating itself; she'd had no mother since early childhood, and now Timmy was without a father. She smiled ruefully, then thrust the thought aside as she placed checked table mats on the counter-top, put out two sets of cutlery and fetched Timmy's feeding-bottle from the fridge.

She had a lot to be thankful for; her father had been so understanding about Timmy. He was the only person to whom she'd confided the full story and had also been the only person to visit her when Timmy was born. There had been no questions, no pressures on her, and she knew she was very lucky in the way he had reacted, and also in the generous allowance he'd insisted on giving her since then.

'Rose! Rose, where are you? Great news!' Melanie's cheerful voice echoed from the hall, bringing a lift to Rose's spirits. She paused in the act of taking Timmy from his cot as her friend hurried into the living-room, hurling a carrier bag of books on to the table before sinking back on to the settee.

'Phew, isn't it hot? I thought I'd die in class today, it was so stuffy. No, don't say it.' Melanie held up an admonitory hand. '"It's not nearly as hot as the desert was this time last year."'

'I wasn't going to say any such thing,' Rose said huffily, nuzzling at the soft sweet-smelling warmth of Timmy's neck.

'I know you weren't. Don't mind me,' Melanie apologised. 'I've had a pig of a day. But wait till you hear my news!'

'Go on, don't keep me in suspense!' Rose sat down beside her friend, her still sleepy son snuggled in her arms. Gently she pushed the surprisingly thick dark hair away from his forehead, hair that was a complete contrast to her own red-gold locks.

'Oh, you're lucky, having such a good baby.' Melanie rested an arm on Rose's shoulder and the friends gazed at Timmy, who stared back wide-eyed, his serious expression lightened by a soft bubble that appeared at the corner of his mouth.

'Well, he may not have a father, but I reckon he's the one that's lucky, with his mum and substitute mum,' laughed Rose, feeling a gush of love for Timmy that almost threatened to suffocate her. 'And if you don't tell me your news, I'll burst!'

'I've been offered a senior staff nurse's post on the children's ward when I finish my exams!'

'But. . .but,' Rose stammered, 'I thought you wanted to get back to be nearer your home.'

'Well,' Melanie looked suddenly shy, 'there are attractions in this part of Surrey, quite apart from the job.'

'Does that mean you want to stay on here at the flat?' Rose squealed in delight, bringing a whimper of protest from Timmy.

'Well, if you'd like me to—it would suit me very well.'

'Of course I'd like you to, you idiot. I can't think of anything nicer. We're lucky that we've always got on so well.'

'Ever since you covered up for me in Theatre when I fainted,' laughed Melanie, her fair curly hair springing out around her face.

'Well, it wasn't surprising you passed out. I'd been working there for some time, and even I still felt queasy when there was an amputation,' Rose said sympathetically.

'I'd have been all right if I'd known about the horrible sawing noise when they cut through the femur. Poor old chap!' Melanie shuddered. 'I can remember how awful his gangrenous foot looked when they took off the dressing.'

'Well, that's all a long time ago, in our young and carefree days,' sighed Rose. A sudden thought struck her. 'What's this other attraction?'

'I hope you'll meet him soon. No, no more questions now.' Melanie held up her hand. 'You see to Timmy and I'll organise the rest of the supper.'

'Oh, I've been asked to do a nurse escort job tomorrow,' said Rose. 'Is that all right?'

'Fine by me.' Melanie bent forward and gently rubbed Timmy's nose with her own. 'We'll go to the park and feed the swans. Perhaps see the cygnets as well.'

'Come along in, Rose, I'm glad you could make it. You look very nice.' Alan stared approvingly at Rose's full-skirted blue and white dress as he put a hand on her waist and ushered her towards the front of the conference-room.

'How's Mr Richards after the tests for his heart problems?' Rose seized Alan's sleeve, stopping him in his tracks.

'I rang yesterday, and he's fine. No more bleeding from his groin, where the catheter had been.' Alan looked at her sympathetically. 'Must have been very frightening.'

'Whew, I should say so!' Rose agreed in heartfelt tones. 'One minute he was happily holding the dressing in place, the next thing he tells me it's all warm. I couldn't believe it when I saw all that blood.'

'I think he must have had something like Warfarin in the past to stop his blood clotting and that's the reason for the haemorrhage,' said Alan. 'I've never heard of anyone reacting like that after a cardiology X-ray, even though we know it's a possibility. You coped very well.'

'Well, I think we broke all records getting the ambulance and patient back to the department. I haven't seen Dave drive like that before,' Rose grinned, remembering the hectic journey.

'Sorry, I must get on with the meeting. How's Timmy?' Not waiting for an answer, Alan patted her arm, then moved past the rows of rapidly filling chairs, where the chatter of ambulance and nursing staff was reaching a crescendo of noise that made Rose blink.

'Just a second, Alan.' She swung round. 'I'll sit at the back, if you don't mind, then if I should have to leave early for some reason, I won't disturb anyone.'

'Suit yourself,' Alan shrugged, his mop of greying hair as untidy as always, his uniform tunic straining on his broad shoulders. 'I must get the rest of the bits and pieces set out. Talk to you later, when we have lunch.' He hurried towards the small platform as Rose sat thankfully in one of the black moulded chairs at the rear. Timmy had been unusually restless the previous night and she wasn't too sure that she'd be able to keep awake throughout the day's proceedings.

But her worries were unnecessary, for there was an updated defibrillator, which was reputed to cause less interference with aircraft radio equipment, a spring balance that could be used to keep tension on spinal neck injuries, and the laughter that accompanied some of the efforts with a new folding stretcher kept not only Rose alert but everyone else as well.

'Right!' Alan called above the hubbub of voices as the discussion became ever noisier, Rose enjoying it as much as anyone. Dearly as she loved Timmy, she found the stimulus of adult company at the agency a welcome break, and it was this as much as her salary that encouraged her to stay available for the occasional escort work.

'Right!' Alan called again. 'Please help yourselves to coffee, the urns are on the table at the back, then we'll be arriving at the important part of the meeting, the introduction of our new medical director.' There was a buzz of wondering comment, before a scramble to collect cups of coffee, dispensed as usual by Alan's long-suffering wife, Marjorie.

'How are you?' Rose held out her cup to be filled, and smiled her thanks, as Marjorie whispered a hurried, 'Fine, and you and Timmy?' before turning to the next person in the line.

Stirring at her cup, Rose moved away from the table, but then couldn't prevent a startled cry as her heel sank into something; she glanced down to see a leather-stitched moccasin beside her own sandalled foot. There was a sharp intake of breath, then a muttered curse in her ear.

'I'm terribly sorry.' Crimson with embarrassment, Rose turned to face the person she had unwittingly trodden on, subconsciously aware of a drift of lemon-sharp cologne.

'You! But it can't be!' she gasped. Every shred of colour drained from her face, leaving it as white as alabaster.

'Are you all right?' The man stared at her, his expression mystified, as Rose blindly felt for a chair and sank on to it, unable to control a violent shaking that rattled her cup in its saucer, and spilt coffee on to her skirt. 'Are you all right?' he repeated. 'You look as though you've seen a ghost!' He smiled in an attempt at reassurance. 'I don't usually have this effect on people when I meet them!'

Rose barely heard him. In fact, all the voices in the room seemed to come from a distance. She was in a bubble that separated her from everything and everyone, a bubble that was as cold as ice.

'Take deep breaths,' the man commanded, placing an encouraging arm around her shoulders. 'Could I get you a drink of water or another coffee, or something else, perhaps?'

It couldn't be him, it couldn't! her mind screamed silently. He was. . .was. . .the thoughts tumbled in her head like the shapes in a kaleidoscope, forming patterns that made no sense. She realised that he'd taken her cup and brought her another with fresh coffee. A large white handkerchief appeared in her hand, she wasn't sure how, and she dabbed uncertainly at the stains on her skirt.

If it was him, why didn't he say something? He

must have recognised her in return. For she knew it was no ghost that stood beside her chair, but a solid man, one that she'd known only too well.

'Rose, are you all right?' Alan's anxious face appeared in front of her as gradually the blurred outlines around her cleared. 'I see you've already met Nick. Trust him to be taking care of the prettiest girl in the room!' he whispered softly.

'I'm Nick Coleman, the new medical director of the company. I didn't catch your name, I'm afraid.'

'Rose—Rose Maslen.' Holding her breath, Rose waited for some comment, some flicker of recognition. But his expression didn't change. Gradually her whirling thoughts settled into a calmer rhythm. If he wanted to continue with this charade, she would have to play along with it. But the fact that he acted as though they were strangers made the shock of seeing him so much worse.

Everyone had finished their coffee and returned their cups, which Marjorie stacked on the table with a clatter that provided a rattling accompaniment in the background.

'Well, Rose Maslen, do you want to rest quietly, or would you prefer that one of us sees you home?'

Rose realised that Nick's words were meant to be soothing, but though his tone was gentle, every sound of his voice seemed like a tiny hammer, striking at her nerves.

She took a deep breath and for the first time stared directly at him. The olive skin was lighter than she remembered, the eyes still dark and smouldering, with finely webbed lines at the corners.

On one side of his forehead was a thin white scar that added to his exotic appearance. He had lost weight, the planes of his face much more sharply defined, but somehow it made him even more attractive, though he hadn't the predatory look about him that she remembered so well.

'I'll be all right. You'd better get back to the platform, I think Alan is waiting for you.' Rose felt quite proud at how calm she now sounded. 'I think I'll just rest here, and if I feel faint again I'll slip out through the back door.' She was relieved to see that, apart from Alan, no one else seemed to have noticed her meeting with Nick.

'If you're sure.' His expression concerned, he moved towards the platform, and Rose felt another lurch seize at her inside. His walk hadn't changed at all, a tigerish lope that somehow didn't look out of place, even with the beautifully tailored tan jacket and stone-coloured trousers that he wore.

CHAPTER TWO

ROSE switched on the television and sank back on to the settee, grateful to be alone in the flat with just her son. She had been unable to face the rest of the meeting at the office and, when the opportunity arose, slipped out and swiftly drove home, her little yellow Beetle close around her like a cocoon. She'd not felt faint again, but the shock of her meeting with Nick Coleman had disturbed her so much, she desperately needed time to herself. Though Melanie had offered to spend the evening at home, Rose had heaved a sigh of relief as she managed eventually to shoo her friend through the door.

Now, showered and dressed in a jade-green tracksuit, for she still felt cold despite the lingering warmth of the day's sunshine, she sat hugging her knees, not focusing on the television, the voice of the commentator merely a background to her thoughts.

Almost like a series of slides, pictures so much more vivid than those in front of her flickered into her mind.

The first was a desert landscape, consisting not only of sweeps of sand, but scrubby bushland, small shrubs and stunted trees dried in the wind that blew incessantly as the battered truck stuttered on its way.

She saw again the clearing in the scrub, camouflaged tents dotted among the few trees, where the sun dappled the ground. In one of those tents was Rose's patient, Jacinta, a young girl with beautiful dark eyes, her badly burnt legs covered with makeshift dressings.

Rose could feel again the horror she'd known when the sound of gunfire had crept nearer and they'd not been able to get back to the air ambulance.

The trek over the next two weeks merged into one long blur, when each day could have been their last. At the centre was the figure of the man who had kept the little group together, his magnetic personality a focus, a pivot on which every one of them depended.

Her crackling awareness of Nico was as vivid in memory as it had been in reality, her sensations sharpened during a short interlude when they were able to rest. The sweep of grassy plains had been cool at night, nights punctuated by the sounds and smells of the big cats and the occasional cackle of a hyena.

Rose rested her chin on her knees, her expression dreamy, sniffing a remembered pungency of campfires. The scent blended in her thoughts with the soft velvet night sky lit by a giant orange moon low on the horizon, when she and Nico had talked incessantly, laughed together and finally made love, every sense heightened by their danger.

Rose had been terrified during the helicopter flight. She never did discover how the message had been sent for the machine to meet them. One early morning, before the harsh African sun had burnt all the dew from the ground and the smells around them were sharp, there had been a clatter in the sky which broke through the soft pearly light. She and Jacinta were whisked away; her last sight of Nico was an arrogant stance, his arm raised in a salute of farewell, scarcely visible through the blurring of her tear-filled eyes.

The sudden small cry from her son brought her abruptly to the present. Scrambling from the settee, she hurried through to the large bedroom at the rear of the flat and swept him into her arms. His soft gummy smile soothed her churned-up feelings, and quickly she changed his sleep suit for a fresh one, its soft lemon colour a contrast to his dark hair and eyes. Gently she carried him through to the sitting-room and put him on a soft blue rug on the floor.

Placing a fluffy ball near his constantly waving arms, she slid open the drawer of an old-fashioned bureau and pulled out a flat cigar box. The lid was stiff to open as she took out a bundle of papers.

'Let's see, Timmy, exactly what it says.' The creases in the blue airmail envelope were grubby with frequent handling. Holding her breath, Rose slipped the single sheet from inside.

'Dear Nurse Rose.' The spidery handwriting was blurred and no easier to read after all these months, but it didn't matter to her, for Rose knew every phrase by heart. Gently her lips shaped the words. 'Please forgive my poor English. I break my heart to tell you Dr Nico is no more with us. There was a mortar attack.' The next few words were illegible, smudged by a stain. 'A million thanks for the care of my sister Jacinta. Perhaps we may meet again. *Inshallah*.'

Sighing deeply, Rose folded the sheet. The signature was also illegible, but the message was clear. 'Dr Nico is no more with us.' But he was very much alive, looked well and, she was afraid, still had the same power over her heart.

'Oh, Timmy,' she muttered somewhere between a laugh and a sob, 'I know how to cope with grieving—I learned all that on the course. Goodness knows, I went through it in person, and if it hadn't been for you it would have taken me a lot longer to recover. But what am I going to do now?' She picked up her son and sniffed at his sweet baby smell, tears trembling on the edge of her lashes. 'No one explained how to cope with bereavement in reverse. And why didn't Nico recognise me?' She stood and glanced in the mirror. Her eyes stared back, huge grey-blue shadows in her creamy white skin; her hair was longer these days and, since Timmy's birth, her figure fuller, but otherwise she hadn't changed that much; had she?

She went into the kitchen and put Timmy's bottle to warm, swinging her son in her arms and comforted by his gurgles of delight.

'Melanie's right, you certainly are a good-tempered baby; I must stop feeling sorry for myself. . .' Her words were interrupted by the sound of the doorbell. Holding Timmy close, Rose went back to the sitting-room and peered round the edge of the curtain. She wasn't expecting anyone and was tempted to ignore the caller, for she would make very bad company, the way she felt at the moment. A large white BMW was parked outside, a car not known to her. Carefully she moved the curtain a little further in the bay window until she could see the visitor waiting on the step.

'Oh, God, what's he doing here?' Hurriedly Rose moved back inside the flat, her heart pounding at the unexpected sight of Nick, still dressed as he had been at the meeting, a large bunch of flowers grasped in one hand.

I'll ignore him, then he'll go away, she thought. Almost running to her bedroom, Rose rested for a moment on the edge of the bed. There was another peremptory ring and she realised her own car was parked just outside. Would Nick know it was hers? Again the bell sounded, her caller pressing continuously against the button so that the noise shrilled through the flat and into her head like toothache.

Quickly she set Timmy in his cot, ran into the sitting-room and cleared the rug from the floor, then, smoothing her hair, slowly opened the door and looked out.

'Oh, thank goodness! I saw the car there, wondered if it was yours and thought you might have felt ill again.' Nick paused, staring down at her, and she noticed how tightly he gripped the bunch of roses. So he wasn't completely at ease, despite the casual way his other hand rested on the door-frame. The realisation that he might be unsure increased her own confidence, and with a smile she stood back and ushered him in.

'I hope you don't mind — Alan gave me your address. He did intend to come and see you himself but had a call to collect a patient from the airport, a myocardial infarction I think it was, coming in from Alicante, and there was no one else to cover. I volunteered to come and see you instead. Oh, these are for you.' He thrust the flowers into her hand. 'Don't be afraid to take them, I've removed all the thorns.'

'It's very kind of you to bother. Sit down.' Rose took the flowers, breathing deeply at their perfume, and rested them on the table, then perched on one of the upright chairs as Nick sank back on to the settee.

'Would you like a coffee?' She wasn't surprised at how disorientated she felt. Her visitor appeared to her in double focus, like the superimposed shadow on a television screen. One image was of the person she had met in East Africa, during their hazardous journey. The other was of this smoothly dressed man, who leaned back apparently relaxed in her tiny flat, clasping his ankle as it rested on the other knee.

'Have you fully recovered? You had us worried, you looked so pale. What was it, a tummy bug?'

'Something like that, I expect.' Rose felt an unexpected glow at the thought of Nick's concern. 'I'm fine now. Would you like a coffee, or I've got some chilled white wine in the fridge?'

'A glass of wine would go down very well, if you're sure I'm not being a nuisance.' He got to his feet and Rose moved back, fearful that he might brush against her in the narrow space of the sitting-room. She couldn't face the thought of even the most trivial contact, at least until she had had time to sort out her feelings. If Nick noticed her involuntary movement, he gave no sign.

'Do you mind if I take off my jacket? It's amazing, but I still find it warm here, despite being in the Sudan and Kenya for so long.'

'Please, be my guest.' Swallowing hard, Rose excused herself and hurried to the kitchen. Why had he visited her? Was he about to explain what had happened to him, and why he was treating her as a stranger? And if he did say anything, should she mention Timmy? Her thoughts scurried to and fro as she set a tray with a bottle of wine and glasses and added some savoury biscuits in a dish. To her relief, a rapid peep in the bedroom revealed that Timmy had fallen asleep. She would wait and see how the evening developed before saying too much about herself or her son.

'That looks very welcome. I haven't interrupted any previous arrangements, have I?' Quickly Nick stood as she returned, taking the tray from her and setting it on the coffee table. She smelt a drift of lemon-sharp cologne, almost overwhelming in its familiarity, as he leant towards her.

'No, I was only having a quiet evening at home.' Not looking at him, Rose poured the wine and passed him a glass, taking her own and sitting again on an upright chair.

'Cheers.' Gravely Nick raised his drink in a gesture of salute. There was an uncomfortable silence for a moment as he stared around the room.

'Nice flat.' He nodded approvingly.

'How did the rest of the meeting go?' Their words clashed and both gave a shaky laugh.

'You first,' ordered Nick. Without his jacket, he looked cool and relaxed, his short-sleeved shirt showing off slim yet powerful shoulders, his arm stretched out along the back of the settee. Rose wished fervently that she could rest as easily, but coupled with the tension of Nick's presence, she was constantly on edge in case Timmy should cry out. Gulping her wine, she refilled her glass and nibbled nervously at one of the biscuits.

'I was only going to ask about the meeting—very boring,' she murmured apologetically.

'Oh,' Nick gave a sudden grin, 'you think the introduction of the new medical director was going to be boring, do you?' His teeth flashed white, the deep lines in his face emphasised by his smile.

'I didn't mean that at all,' Rose said hurriedly. 'I meant... I meant...' She paused. What had she meant? Her mind was in such a turmoil it was not surprising that she didn't talk sense. She could hardly think coherently, let alone make polite conversation. Take a deep breath, she told herself firmly. Pretend you've just met. It seems to be what Nick intends to do, whatever the reason.

'You said you were in East Africa,' she began. 'Were you working there or just visiting?'

'Working. I must say, despite a lot of problems, I really enjoyed my time there.' His eyes were partly closed in thought, their rich dark brown colour hidden. 'It's possibly not to everyone's taste, but

Africa's a wonderful continent and has so much to offer. In spite of famines and civil wars, East Africa does things to you. Or it suits me, anyway.' He sipped at his glass, then looked at her. 'Have you ever been there?'

Rose could feel a trembling start inside. Yes, I have, she thought sharply, and it led to one of the most devastating times of my life. A sudden spurt of resentment welled up inside her, but to her relief, when she finally spoke her voice was steady.

'I did go once, to do a medical pick-up, but I didn't really have enough time to visit the country properly,' she told him.

'That's a pity. You must try and go again if you get the chance. Parts of Kenya, particularly the Highlands, have some of the most beautiful scenery in the world, and the people are so friendly. Even the desert has its own austere attraction, especially at night when the sky is like dark velvet and the stars are almost bright enough to read by. I can definitely recommend it. Anyway, enough of the travelogue.' Nick laughed apologetically. 'Tell me about yourself. How long have you worked for Alan? Are you full-time or what?'

'Would you like some more wine?' Hastily Rose picked up the bottle and refilled his glass, taking the moment to try and collect her thoughts.

'Whoa, that's enough, thank you. I have to drive home. You were saying?'

'Was I?' Rose's tone was pensive. She cleared her throat noisily. 'I've worked for Alan for the past month, but I've known him and Marjorie for years, ever since I was young.'

'And now you're not young, I take it,' Nick teased.

'Age isn't only measured in time; experience counts as well, and I've experienced a lot in my twenty-four years,' Rose said sharply, almost offended at his casual tone. It was incredible that he should be behaving in this way. It didn't help, either, that she was still so physically stirred in his company. She didn't feel the same yearning hunger that she had experienced during their desert journey; at that time she had had to struggle constantly to hold back the attraction she'd felt.

But every part of her was aware of him now and the sensations in her blood stream were as strong, despite her efforts at trying to match his nonchalance.

She suddenly realised that Nick was waiting for her to speak, his expression wary.

'I'm sorry if I said something to upset you,' he smiled tentatively.

'I'm the one who should apologise.' Rose suddenly realised how abrupt she'd sounded. 'Tell me more about your time in Africa, please. Oh, is there something wrong?' For Nick winced as he bent forward to pick up his glass from the table.

'No, just a slight headache. It comes and goes. It's a legacy of this little problem.' He pointed to the scar on his forehead.

'Can I get you some Paracetamol?' She jumped up from the chair, but he leant towards her and pulled her on to the settee beside him.

'I'm fine,' he assured her.

'What happened? Was it an accident?'

'What is it the comic books say?' Suddenly Nick laughed loudly. 'It's an old war wound.'

'I'm sorry, I didn't mean to pry.' Stiffly Rose edged away from him, staring straight ahead.

'I don't mind your asking. I really was injured, in an explosion caused by mortar fire. It was my own fault; I was where I shouldn't have been. I can't give you any more details, for my mind is a blank about the time leading up to the injury. I'd been transferred to a hospital in Kenya, and woke up there not knowing where I was or what had happened. It's a very funny sensation, I can tell you — a part of your life missing.' He paused and studied Rose's shocked expression, his eyes shadowy with concern.

'Please, don't look so horrified! It's all behind me now, and I'm as good as new. Hey, your hands are as cold as ice. Are you feeling ill again?'

Dumbly Rose shook her head.

'I don't usually confide all my past life to someone on first acquaintance, but it's funny, isn't it? With some people there's often an immediate affinity — almost as though you'd known them before. I feel I can talk easily to you.' He looked into her eyes. 'Are you sure you're all right?' Quickly he released her hands and stood. 'Point me towards the kitchen and I'll get us some coffee.'

'No, please don't bother. I'll be fine in a minute, but I think I would like an early night.' The last thing she wanted was for him to go through to the rear of the flat and inadvertently discover Timmy.

She needed time to think over what he'd told her, for her mind was now in a greater state of turmoil than ever.

'Of course, if you're sure there's nothing I can get you.' Nick moved across the room and picked up his jacket. In the quiet that followed, Rose heard a small but distinct noise from the bedroom.

'I'm sorry,' she gabbled nervously. She was too confused to understand why, but she definitely didn't want Nick to know anything about Timmy, at least not yet. 'I don't feel very well after all. Would you think me very rude if I asked you to go?'

Nick shook his head. 'Of course not. I didn't mean to outstay my welcome. Are you sure there's nothing I can get you?'

Again Rose shook her head, not trusting herself to say any more.

'Well then,' he continued, 'if you aren't too busy one evening, perhaps we could go out for a meal.' He picked up her left hand and studied it. 'I take it you're not married or engaged or anything?'

'No, I'm not, and I'll be happy to. . .' Heavens, she thought anxiously as another sound reached her, I wish he'd just leave. Swiftly she pulled her hand from his grasp as the sound of Timmy's cry from the rear of the flat increased in volume. Surely he must hear it? Almost pushing him ahead of her, Rose opened the front door. As Nick paused, shrugging his arm into the sleeve of his jacket, a fluffy ball fell to the ground and she felt her heart sink.

'I think this must belong to you. Been baby-sitting, have you? I'll be in touch.' Shaking her firmly by the hand, Nick went out through the front door and turned to wave as he reached his car. There was still a glow in the evening sky, and Rose felt her heart stir at the sight of him. For his salute was an exact replica of the time they had parted before her flight in the helicopter. And her thoughts and memories tumbled in her head in a confusion that made her feel almost faint again as she shut the front door. What was going to be the outcome of Nick's return to her life?

But she hadn't time to think of it just now, for her son was obviously offended at being left, his cries a roar echoing through the flat. Running to the bedroom, she felt a surge of guilt at her brief neglect and swung the baby into her arms; as she hugged him close, with soft murmurs of comfort, she thought again how much he resembled his father. Timmy's large dark eyes gazed back at her, so like those of the man who had just left.

'Come on, Timmy — to make up for leaving you to cry, we'll have an extra playtime.' Kissing him again on the cheek, she held him close and returned to the sitting-room.

'Damn!' The telephone's peremptory ring cut into her game with her son, and she sighed as she picked up the receiver.

'Hello, Rose, it's Alan. Is Nick still with you?'

'No, I'm afraid he left a few minutes ago.'

There was an apologetic cough from the other end of the line. 'Sorry, Rose, I forgot to ask. Are you feeling better?'

Absent-mindedly, she nodded, her mind for a

moment on Timmy's antics. He was already trying to turn on to his back, though she had placed him firmly on his stomach as the telephone started to ring.

'Are you there?' A touch impatiently, Alan's voice reached her again.

'Sorry, Alan, I was miles away. I'm fine now. How was your patient?'

'Oh, we delivered him safely to Brighton. His heart problem wasn't as bad as we'd been led to believe, though he had quite a few abnormal rhythms on the return flight. Anyway, I'd better see if I can get hold of Nick. I'm not too sure if he's had the phone put in at his new house as yet.'

'Alan, before you go, can I ask a favour?' said Rose. 'Would you mind not telling Nick about Timmy at present?'

'Well, if you don't want me to.' Alan's tone was doubtful. 'You've got nothing to be ashamed of, you know. After all, it wasn't your fault that Timmy's father was killed before Timmy was born. You've been very brave in the way you've coped with everything during the past year.'

'Well, it's nice of you to say so. I couldn't have done it without the help that you and Marjorie have given me. But I'd still rather not mention it for the time being.' A short thrill of guilt went through her, for she had not told even Alan and his wife the full story, but she had found it impossible to discuss it at the time, and somehow her half-lie had gone on so long, it now had every appearance of truth.

'All right, I'll see what I can do. You realise it could get complicated, don't you?'

'I know, and I'm sorry to ask such a thing. But it means a lot to me. One day I'll be able to tell you the whole story.' At least, I hope I will, her thoughts cut in doubtfully, for she wasn't really sure how she could attempt to explain her relationship to Nick.

'Was Nick all right this evening?' asked Alan.

'Yes. Any reason why he shouldn't have been?' Rose blinked uncertainly at the question.

'It's just that he was blown up during some fighting while working in the Sudan last year. He lost consciousness for a while and was lucky not to sustain any permanent damage. But he still gets quite bad headaches.' Alan paused.

'He did tell me a bit about it,' she admitted.

'Did he indeed?' Alan sounded surprised. 'You're honoured! He doesn't very often confide details of his personal life.'

'What details would those be?' Rose cut in anxiously. Surely Nick didn't have a commitment to someone else? Though she couldn't imagine him asking her out if he had.

'He also has another problem, in that he has some loss of memory, particularly about the time leading up to the explosion. Not that it affects his work, of course.'

'Mmm, he mentioned that as well. I thought he was making fun when he said it was an old war wound.'

'Oh, that's just his way of dealing with it. I think he was quite shocked that he couldn't remember—he's the sort who's always in control, or so I've been told. And anyway, he could have done all sorts and not known anything about it, couldn't he? What's the matter?' Alan added at Rose's audible gasp. 'Are you all right, Rose?' he repeated. 'You didn't mind that Nick came to see you instead of me, did you? We were both very concerned at how poorly you looked.'

'Of course not. I thought it was very nice of him to bother.'

'And there's nothing else you want to tell me? You sound strained, even now. Don't forget, I'm supposed to keep an eye on you—I promised your father I would.' Alan's deep rumbling laugh echoed on the line. 'Anyway, to change the subject, how are you fixed for duty next week?'

'I can manage some shifts, I expect.' Rose forced a laugh in return. 'I could do with the money, with the way Timmy's growing. I think he's already cutting a tooth.'

'Marjorie and I must come and see our godson again soon. Well, time to go. Bye for now.'

Thoughtfully Rose replaced the receiver. Nick really had lost his memory. It explained so many things. Such as why he'd been acting as though she were a stranger.

A sudden shaft of light seemed to fill the room. 'Timmy,' she cried, 'just imagine, I didn't suspect it at all at first. How could I have been so stupid. . .?' She stopped abruptly.

'But that means I can't tell him about Timmy at all,' she whispered harshly. 'If he doesn't remember me, I daren't say a word. Goodness knows what he'd make of the news that he has a son he knows nothing about.'

Her eyes opened wide in horror as another thought came to mind. 'He might even think I'm trying to trap him into some sort of relationship. Thank heavens I asked Alan not to say anything!'

Timmy gurgled happily as though he understood every word of her agonised musings, then managed to roll on to his back. Rose rushed to rescue him, for his smooth dark head came perilously close to the chair leg.

'Perhaps I'd better explain about you to Alan,' she murmured to her son. 'I've a horrible suspicion that coping with the details of your parenthood is going to get more and more complicated. Oh, hell!' she said loudly. 'Why, oh, why did this have to happen, when we'd at least got some sort of pattern into our lives?'

She paused. 'Ye gods,' she whispered softly, 'that sounds as though I'm sorry that Nick's still alive. Of course I'm not—I'm not, Timmy.' She smiled a twisted smile. 'But I can see stormy waters ahead.'

At that moment Timmy interrupted her with a squeal of frustration as he tried unsuccessfully to pull one bare foot towards his mouth. 'It's all right for you—you've got nothing to worry about except your next bottle and your next dry nappy!' she smiled. 'Still, whatever happens, at least I've got you, and that's something I wouldn't change, whatever the future brings.'

CHAPTER THREE

'WATCH his head! Careful with the traction! Whatever you do, don't release the weights until I tell you.' Nick spat out the orders in rapid succession as the three of them, doctor, nurse and paramedic, moved carefully round the bed, where their patient, a young man with a neck injury, lay. The prongs of large metal tongs were set into each side of his head, just above the ears. Weights from the apex of the tongs, suspended on a pulley over the head of the bed, extended his neck as he lay absolutely still.

'How unstable is the injury?' Rose muttered nervously to the Intensive Care Unit sister, a tall woman with thick dark hair, who hovered round them like a mother with one chick.

'Very unstable,' she said sharply. 'Peter has an injury of the cervical spine, and really I think it's a little shortsighted, arranging a scan at the Central hospital. Surely they could wait until our scanner is repaired? It's only putting him at risk of paralysis.' Her eyes sparkled angrily, and Rose could understand her concern. It was one of the most difficult transport jobs Fleetline had been asked to do, to take the patient to a nearby hospital for further scanning. To all intents and purposes, his neck was partially dislocated. Any disturbance of the spinal cord could, as Sister pointed out, risk a permanent paralysis.

Rose had been a little taken aback to discover that in addition to herself, Alan and a paramedic, Nick was also to be travelling with them. But she shouldn't have been surprised, she told herself, for she knew that during the past week, since his appointment to Fleetline, he had spent at least some time each day either at the office or on one of the ambulance trips.

'Wouldn't it be easier for Peter to travel by helicopter, rather than by road?' she asked Alan as they carefully rolled Peter on to a vacuum mattress that, when the air was withdrawn, would mould itself around his body. Sister hovered nervously, then insisted on supporting the weights at the head of the bed herself. Keeping Peter's body in line, Alan, Nick and Rose transferred their patient to the stretcher.

One false move, Rose thought anxiously, her teeth aching with concentration during the lift, and that's it.

'A helicopter wouldn't be of use here,' Nick muttered, having heard her query. 'The nearest available place suitable for a landing is almost as far as the whole journey by road, so there wouldn't be any benefit. Anyway,' he murmured softly, 'as you can see, Peter is nervous enough at the thought of being moved. A helicopter would probably scare him even more.'

Rose looked again at Peter, his face dominated by

a pair of huge blue eyes, which followed every move they made.

It must make it worse for him because he can't talk at the moment with his tracheostomy, she thought sympathetically. Nick was right, there was an edge of terror underlying Peter's feeble attempt at a smile.

'I know this may sound stupid, but try not to worry, you're going to be all right. We'll make sure of that,' she whispered softly as the little caravan of staff moved through the door, followed by an anxious, 'See you later,' from Sister.

'I'll take care of the weights on the outward journey and Dave here can look after them coming back.' Alan gestured with his free hand towards their paramedic at the foot of the stretcher. And to Rose's relief, the lift into their ambulance was accomplished more easily than she expected.

It was cramped in the rear, and she carefully hunched herself well away from Nick. By sticking to the principle of one day at a time, she had built a layer of pleasant friendliness in her relationship with him, and had felt that, even if he didn't remember her from before, at least some of the old attraction was there.

But oh, she sighed softly to herself, as she perched on the small bucket seat beside the stretcher, it was hard at times not to say something, in an effort to jog his memory.

'Doesn't the road look peculiar without any traffic?' She bent forward and looked through the shaded window at the dual carriageway outside; the only other vehicle going in their direction was the police escort car ahead, the sun's reflection dazzling on its polished roof.

'You're like royalty, Peter,' Rose told their patient, holding his hand in a comforting clasp. 'Did you know that the road has been closed to all other traffic?'

He raised his eyebrows in a gesture of surprise, then mouthed a thank-you as she wiped his face with a damp cloth.

'It must have taken some organising.' She turned to Alan, who sat at the head of the stretcher, his large capable hands supporting the traction weights with no apparent strain.

'Well, I wasn't too sure that it could be arranged, but Nick had no doubts at all. And I must admit,' he grinned at the medical director, who sat quietly in the other seat, keeping a careful eye on the portable ventilator and heart monitor, 'when I listened to him, I guessed that no one would be able to resist him, not even the most stony-hearted bureaucrat.'

'You would have done just as well,' Nick smiled in return. Rose glanced in his direction, aware of a quality she'd noticed during their time in East Africa. Despite his looking totally relaxed there was nothing restful in the way he sat. Instead, an underlying feeling of controlled power came from him. And as she studied the crisp white shirt that sat snugly on his shoulders and the smooth grey slacks above black casual shoes, she could feel his magnetism so strongly, she was surprised that no one else in the ambulance could read her thoughts.

Their route had been carefully chosen to avoid other major traffic areas, and, even driving at a rate that seemed incredibly slow, it wasn't long before they arrived at the Central Hospital with its scanner building clearly signposted inside the main gate.

'I hope there aren't any sleeping policemen on our route,' muttered Nick as they edged into the hospital drive. 'We need no lumps or bumps now.'

His hopes were realised, a smooth tarmac drive providing an easy ride, and it wasn't long before the ambulance backed carefully into position in front of blue-painted double doors.

The lift on to a stretcher to take Peter to the scanner was carried out as successfully as the previous one. But Rose realised how tense she had been when the ambulance crew were able to leave Peter for a few minutes and enjoy a pot of coffee, thoughtfully provided by the radiographers.

'I must say, this is very civilised.' Alan slurped energetically at his mug before topping it up. 'Any more for anyone?' He held the pot aloft.

'Not for me.' There was a concerted shake of heads, before Nick moved away to study the computer read-outs that were flashing up on the screen by this time.

'Whew, come and look at this!' Reaching out behind him, Nick took Rose by the arm and led her to the bank of computers pointing to the pictures looking similar to X-rays that gradually appeared on the screen. 'It's a wonder that Peter wasn't paralysed at the time of the accident. Just look at the distortion in the cervical cord!'

He rested an arm lightly on her shoulder and gestured towards the computer, which she stared at with every appearance of absorbed attention. But each nerve she possessed was conscious of the feel of his body pressed close to hers and the aroma that drifted from his skin, a masculine essence combined with the familiar lemon-sharp cologne.

Evocatively, the smell of him brought a vivid picture to her mind, a memory of one evening on their trek. They had been hurrying throughout the day and finally found a suitable place to camp. Rose had been shaking as she sat on the ground, partly from tension, partly from fatigue, and Nico had pulled her to her feet to take her to the edge of the small clearing.

He had pressed alongside her to point out a lion cub, in much the same way as he was almost resting his cheek against hers now, and she turned to face him, swamped in memory.

A gentle sigh left her half-parted lips, her eyes gazed into his with a yearning she couldn't hide. There was a half-smile on his face as his sherry-coloured eyes stared deep into her own, which at the same time didn't disguise his look of bewilderment.

'How's the CAT scan coming along?' Guiltily, Rose swung round to face a surprised-looking Alan. Despite his bulk, she had not heard his approach, and she knew the smile she attempted must have looked very forced.

'I think they've nearly finished.' Casually, Nick picked up the films and laid them on the desk. 'We should be able to see about transferring Peter back to his own comfortable bed.' He was calm, neither his voice nor his expression showing any sign of embarrassment.

'I'll see if Peter would like a drink.' Hastily Rose picked up a cup, begged a straw from one of the X-ray staff and hurried to the stretcher where her patient was waiting.

'All right, Peter?' She prayed her hand wouldn't shake as she held the straw to his lips, for her insides were churning so much, she felt as though she could hardly breathe. If Alan hadn't turned up just then, she would have betrayed herself to Nick, she knew it! She must be on her guard the whole time in his company. It might even be better to keep well away from him, for the time being. After all, she'd managed her life very well without him for the past year. It shouldn't be too difficult to do so again.

'Is that enough?' Peter blinked his expressive eyes in answer to her query, looking much less worried than he'd been during his trip.

'Not too bad, was it? And we'll soon have you back at your own hospital. What did you say?' Carefully Rose watched his lips as he shaped the words with exaggerated care. 'You won't be sorry? No, I'm sure you won't.' She smiled reassuringly. And neither will I, she thought, looking towards the bank of computer screens and her colleagues. Nick was discussing the films with a shorter middle-aged man in a white coat as Alan and Dave waited quietly to one side.

Rose tried hard to look anywhere but at Alan. Whatever must he have thought, when he'd seen

Nick and herself just now? Perhaps she should confide in Alan about her previous relationship with Nick? Though if she did, it would only put the burden of her secret on to his shoulders and, broad though they were, she didn't feel it was fair to him or Marjorie.

Though if I carry on gazing at Nick like some dewy-eyed virgin, she told herself angrily, I'll be the only one to blame if he begins to wonder what's going on.

'Come on, everyone, time to get back.' Briskly, Alan gripped the end of the stretcher and steered it on its thick rubber wheels carefully through the door, leaving Nick to collect the films and notes belonging to their patient.

'Do you want to sit in the back, or would you rather ride up front this time?' His eyebrows raised questioningly, Alan stood beside the open ambulance doors as Nick and Dave settled the stretcher and all the equipment in place.

'I'll ride in the back, of course.' Without a backward glance, Rose climbed up the two steps into the rear of the ambulance and, as she had on the outward journey, clasped Peter's hand firmly in her own long fingers. Nick barely acknowledged her as she sat in the bucket seat once more, and she was grateful that she could use the excuse of being on the far side of the stretcher from him and stare out of the window as Alan carefully drove away from the double doors of the prefabricated building.

'Are you comfortable?' she whispered to her

patient, and was rewarded with a smile of surprising sweetness. 'Not so nervous this time? Good.'

'I think you've been marvellous.' Nick bent across, reaching to adjust the flow of the tiny ventilator, whose rhythmic click-click always reminded Rose of a metronome. 'I've had a good look at the scan films, and I know your own surgeon will tell you the same as me: that the swelling in your spinal cord,' he rested a gentle finger at the back of Peter's neck, 'seems to be settling nicely. How much movement have you got?'

Peter wriggled his fingers, an expression of fierce concentration on his face. Then with a cheeky grin he shifted one foot slightly and slid it along the stretcher.

'Is that more than you could do at the time of the accident?'

Peter's special look of agreement flashed across his face.

He communicates amazingly well, thought Rose, lost in admiration for the twenty-two-year-old who could so easily have been completely paralysed by his motorcycle accident.

'I'm sure I wouldn't have been as patient,' Nick continued. 'I was in an accident last year and, typical doctor, I was the world's worst!' He smiled disarmingly. 'Wouldn't do as I was told, never believed that what the doctors told me was for my own good—you name the awkwardness a patient can come up with, that was me! So I can appreciate a little bit how frustrating the whole situation must be for you.'

'What are you trying to say?' Rose bent forward and stared intently at Peter's mobile mouth.

'Sorry, I didn't quite catch that. You'd like me to go out with you when you're better? Thank you, I'd be honoured.' She squeezed his hand. 'What? You've always had a weakness for hair this colour? Thanks.' She giggled in delight, relieved that Peter seemed so much more at ease.

'I have to admit to a weakness for that red-gold colour myself. It's lovely, isn't it?' Nick grinned a confidential grin, and Rose prayed he wouldn't notice the blush that stained her face.

'How are you lasting out with the weights, Dave?' Hurriedly she turned towards the silent paramedic, his interest in the conversation apparent from the mischievous twinkle in his deep-set eyes.

'Fine, thanks, Rose. We won't be much longer anyway.'

Shortly afterwards the ambulance turned into the main gate of the hospital and moved at its careful pace towards the door and lift leading to the ITU.

'We're here, Peter,' said Rose. 'I bet Sister will be relieved! I don't think she trusts anyone but herself to take care of you, and I don't blame her.'

'Right, Rose, you go first.' Gently pushing her ahead, Nick sprang lightly down the two steps of the ambulance, then turned and waited as Alan, who had hurried round from the driver's seat, stood alongside.

The three men manoeuvred the stretcher and patient to the ground, every move in slow motion, and wheeled Peter steadily back to the unit.

'All right, Peter?' Trying to disguise her anxiety, Sister bent over the bed as soon as the ambulance personnel had unloaded their precious cargo and took hold of her patient's hand.

'Would you like coffee?' With a smile that lightened her rather stern features, she turned to face Rose and Nick as they stood by the bedside.

'Thank you, Sister, but I think we have to get back to the office. We've several other calls waiting,' answered Nick.

'Goodbye, Peter. Don't forget you owe me a date. I'll be in touch.' Rose blew a kiss before following dutifully in the wake of the stretcher, her hand resting lightly on its rim. Peering from under her lashes, she sneaked a glance in Nick's direction, noticing again how different he seemed from the man she had known in Africa. There was gentleness in his bearing and he seemed careful, both of people's feelings and emotions.

Though the circumstances had been so different previously, of course, with an underlying tension that was difficult to imagine on the calm Surrey roads they were travelling en route back to the office. There he had had so much responsibility, not only medically but also for everyone's safety, and it wasn't surprising that he had seemed to make little allowance for how anyone felt.

Though she might have guessed that he could be gentle, remembering their lovemaking in the soft African nights. Despite the overwhelming passion which had taken them both to unbelievable heights,

Nick had been tender and considerate of her feelings.

She suddenly realised that Nick was studying her closely, an enigmatic expression on his face. She hoped he wasn't able to read her thoughts. Remembering them, she blushed crimson, bowing her head forward in an attempt to cover her face with a veil of hair. Which was impossible, as she'd tied it back in a ponytail before starting duty.

'What's the time?' A glance at her watch brought panic to her face.

'Is something the matter?' queried Nick.

'I have to get home sharp by one.' Anxiously Rose stared out from the window, then groaned aloud. In contrast to their escorted journey of earlier that day, the road ahead now was packed with a slow-moving stream of cars and lorries, jammed together as far ahead as she could see.

'What's causing the hold-up?' She leaned towards Alan and Dave as they sat patiently in the front seat.

'I'm not sure, it's impossible to see from here.' Alan stared sympathetically at her worried expression.

'But Melanie's on second shift. I promised I'd be back by one at the latest.' She fidgeted, worry about Timmy and letting down her friend making her heart beat fast.

'What's the problem?' Nick raised strongly defined eyebrows, his eyes looking searchingly into hers.

'I have to get back home — I just have to!' she told him.

'I'm sorry, there's no way Dave can speed things up. Even if we cut off the dual carriageway, there are roadworks on the Dorking road; it was murder getting along there this morning,' Alan muttered over his shoulder.

'Calm down!' Gently Nick took Rose by the hand. 'It's not essential for you to get back before your friend leaves, is it?'

'Yes, it is,' Rose snapped, pulling her hand free.

'I'll phone her and say you might be late. Is there anyone else. . .?' Alan broke off as the radiophone buzzed. 'Janet, could you ring Rose's flat and tell Melanie she might be late back? Thanks. We've completed our trip to the scanner and safely delivered the patient back to his own hospital, but the traffic's jammed solid as far as we can see, so I'm not sure what time we'll be back. Any problems?'

'Nothing we can't handle.' The disembodied voice squawked back reassuringly.

'I suppose we could be very naughty and use the siren.' Nick gave Alan a quizzical look.

'Wouldn't be much point, to be truthful. Anyway, I don't like to take advantage. . . What?'

'Got a problem?' The deep voice through the open window startled all of them into silence. A motorcycle policeman, looking like some bizarre helmeted insect, peered into the open window.

'We've got to get back to the office. It's not a medical emergency as such, but this hold-up is causing a lot of problems for one of the staff.' Nick leaned forward to the cab and spoke crisply to the officer.

'Causing problems for a lot of people,' the officer replied drily. He paused and stared. 'Aren't you the ambulance that drove that young patient with neck problems this morning?'

Alan nodded.

'That's different. Follow me.' Pulling on his gloves, the policeman wheeled his machine to just in front of the ambulance, signalling to them with his right arm.

Like toothpaste squeezed from a tube, they edged in his wake, throwing up grass seeds and dust as they brushed through the verge, and were soon led to a side road that was mercifully clear.

'I know where we are.' Dave grinned all round. 'I wouldn't have thought of coming this way, but. . .'

He left the rest of his words in the air as the policeman waved them past, giving a salute to the one whine from the siren that Dave allowed himself.

'Well, that was a bit of luck!' Rose sat back in her seat with an enormous sigh. But her relief that they wouldn't be long in returning was lost as Nick leant towards her.

'You're quite a mystery, aren't you? Am I allowed to hear why it was so desperate for you to get back home, or. . .?' He gazed deep into her eyes, a half-smile lifting the corner of his mouth, but Rose shivered as she looked back. There was no smile in his eyes; they were as cold as pieces of slate.

'I was just. . .it's just that. . .' she stammered, staring away from him through the ambulance window. The delicate fabric of their relationship seemed to be in danger of ripping apart, and she was so confused, she couldn't find any good reason other than the genuine one to explain why she'd been in such a hurry. And Nick was obviously — what? Upset? Offended? It wasn't surprising; she'd been very curt just now: as she'd been on the two occasions she refused to go out with him when he'd asked.

Oh, damn and double damn! she thought. Why can my life never be straightforward? But she was saved from saying anything more as the ambulance pulled up outside the office.

Quickly she scrambled down the two steps as Alan opened the rear door.

'Sorry I've got to rush. I'll ring you, Alan. Bye, Nick — bye, Dave.' Not pausing to wait for a reply, she fled across the road to the main car park, flung herself into the driver's seat of her Beetle and set off with a swirl of gravel and exhaust fumes towards her flat and her son.

Impatiently she brushed at the suspicion of moisture that dampened her eyes. It was only the fumes from the traffic, of course. But her heart felt as heavy as lead, at the way Nick had looked at her, at the way he'd gripped her arm and at the distaste that she'd sensed as she so obviously regaled him with half-truths.

'"Oh, what a tangled web",' she snorted, wishing desperately that there were an easy way out of her muddle. But it didn't seem that there was. And everything she tried to do seemed to make the situation ever more unsettled, and her own feelings and wishes ever more confused.

CHAPTER FOUR

BLUE eyes like saucers, Melanie put down her fork and picked up her glass of wine. 'Rose, it's the most romantic thing I've ever heard!'

'Well, I don't know about romantic,' Rose said ruefully. 'I could think of other words to describe it.'

'Do you mean to tell me that Nick has no idea?'

'None at all. Do you want some more salad?' Rose pushed the dish into Melanie's unresponsive hand. 'And don't forget,' she warned, 'you're not to say a word, not even to Alan.'

'But, Rose, how long do you think you can keep this up?' Absently, Melanie put a helping of salad on to her plate and broke her bread roll in two.

The evening sun still shone through the kitchen window of the flat, but a lot of the heat of the past few days had gone and there had been a cold wind at night that threatened the end of summer, although the calendar still said it was July.

Rose had worked very few shifts since her trip with Nick and Alan to take Peter to the scanner, for it had been difficult to arrange times to fit in with Melanie's new job. She was beginning to feel trapped in the flat, her only outings visits to the park with Timmy and a trip to the clinic for his check-up.

'Tell me again.' Impatiently Melanie pushed her

plate away and leant her elbows on the edge of the table.

'You remember last year I did a special flight for that Arabian company? They particularly wanted a female nurse to pick up one of their nationals from near the Sudanese border?' Rose began.

'Yes, I know that,' Melanie interrupted eagerly. 'And while you were there, you were trapped by fighting between rebels and government forces which flared up near you—couldn't get back to the air ambulance or something. Talk about exciting!'

'That's right, we had to find another way out, and the doctor who was the mainstay of our little expedition was one Nico Coleman, also known as Nick, now working for Fleetline.' Rose drained the last drops of wine into her glass and drank thirstily.

'And he really doesn't remember anything about you?'

'Apparently not. The explosion that I thought had killed him has made him lose part of his memory. Leave the dishes, I'll see to them later.'

'Rightio,' said Melanie. 'I'll put the coffee on—would you like some?'

Rose nodded and piled plates and cutlery into a bowl, covering them with cold water. She rested against the edge of the kitchen stool as Melanie filled the kettle and set out two bright blue mugs.

'Instant all right?' queried Melanie.

Rose nodded again, barely noticing. Her thoughts were so mixed-up of late, she didn't know if she was coming or going.

'I've been thinking seriously of giving up at

Fleetline,' she continued as she followed Melanie from the kitchen.

'You can't do that!' Skilfully manoeuvring the tray through the doorway to the sitting-room, Melanie set it on the coffee table and with a smile of triumph pulled out a large box of chocolates from her bag. 'Come on, let's spoil ourselves for once. Present from the grateful parents of a patient.' She ripped open the cellophane wrapping and held out the box for her friend to take a chocolate.

'Funny how patients always give nurses chocolates, isn't it?' Rose managed a wan smile as she bit firmly into a caramel.

'I think it must date back to the old days when nurses were so badly paid and chocolates were a real treat. I'm not complaining, mind you.' Melanie took a mug from the tray and sank back on to the settee.

'Anyway,' Rose grimaced at her friend, 'what am I going to do?'

'First of all, tell Nick you have a baby. It's not something you can keep a secret, especially as he's asked you out a couple of times.'

'But Timmy looks just like him!' Rose moaned. 'There's no mistaking the fact that he's Timmy's father.'

'Then if Nick ever comes here, you must make sure that Timmy is asleep in his cot. Surely that shouldn't be too difficult? Anyway, it may be obvious to you that Timmy looks like Nick, but it doesn't mean to say that Nick would see the likeness,' Melanie pointed out.

'I suppose not,' Rose said doubtfully.

'And the other thing you must do is tell Alan exactly what the situation is. You can trust him to keep Timmy's circumstances a secret.' Melanie paused, studying her friend's face intently. 'You don't regret having Timmy, do you?'

'Of course not! However complicated life gets, I wouldn't be without him for anything. He's the most important thing in my life,' Rose said firmly.

'All right, no need to glare at me like that!' Melanie giggled, and after a moment Rose joined in, and if there was an element of hysteria in the sound of their laughter—well, Rose thought, it's none the worse for that.

'What are the chances of Nick recovering his memory?' Wiping her eyes, Melanie put her cup on the tray and wriggled back more comfortably on to the settee.

'I don't know,' said Rose. 'The only neuro I've done was in Intensive Care, so I've only seen head injuries at the acute stage. What happens in the long term is a closed book to me.'

'Well, I did three months during my training, but I don't know much either. Do you want me to try and find out what I can? There's a staff nurse on my ward who worked in neuro-surgery at one time. I could ask him, if you like.'

'Would you? If I could have some idea how all this muddle will turn out, it would help a lot to cope. After all, what am I supposed to do, if Nick never recovers his memory? Do I keep it a secret for the rest of my life? Just imagine, if he should want to marry someone else?' Rose stopped speaking, a sharp stab of pain going through her at the thought of Nick with another woman. It didn't bear thinking about. Melanie sat in silence, studying her for a moment, then jumped to her feet.

'Here's tonight's paper—let's see what's on the box. If there's nothing you fancy, I'll go and hire a video. We'll just wallow in thoughtless viewing, not worry about your problems anymore tonight.'

'Aren't you going out?' Rose stared at her friend in surprise. 'Saturday night, as well?'

'No—I'm pretty bushed. You'll never believe what a day it's been! We admitted a little boy with query appendicitis and he had a nasty problem with the small bowel, then there was a three-year-old with a head injury, fell from a swing.'

'Don't tell me any more about sick children, please!' Rose shuddered. 'I can't seem to cope with the idea, now that I've got Timmy.'

'Sorry.' Melanie shrugged apologetically. 'It's all very well having the senior staff nurse's post, but I didn't know that Sister Baker was going on holiday just as I started. A quiet evening by the telly will suit me down to the ground.' She put the mugs on to the tray and moved towards the door. 'And while I'm gone, please hide the rest of those chocolates, or I shall sit and stuff them all night long!'

'I thought that was the idea,' laughed Rose, her eyes scanning the list of programmes in the paper. 'Nothing here I fancy—one Australian film, one alternative comedy. . . It's all right,' she called, 'I'll get it.' She threw down the paper and hurried to the front door in answer to the impatient buzz that sounded.

'I'm sorry, but my car's broken down and the telephone box at the corner has been vandalised. Please could I use your phone?'

Rose's heart did a quick flip at the sight of Nick outlined in the glow of the evening sun. His dark hair was ruffled and there was a smudge of oil on one cheek, but still he managed to look cool and self-possessed, his snug-fitting jeans and dark blue sports shirt emphasising the lean grace of his body, his smile of apology a white flash in his olive skin.

'Of course—come in.' She stood back to let him pass, then paused, breathing deeply to try and still her rapidly beating heart. He would call this particular evening, she thought, as she glanced down at her shabby tracksuit trousers, the grey colour almost completely faded and then pulled at the stretched waist of her T-shirt. Well, there was no way she could rush past Nick to the bedroom to change.

And plainly the gods were determined not to let her escape from her problems. With an impatient shrug of her shoulders, she preceded Nick to the sitting-room as Melanie returned from the kitchen.

'Melanie, this is Nick Coleman, the medical director at Fleetline,' she said.

She heard Melanie's small intake of breath in the seconds that followed as she hurried to introduce her friend to their unexpected visitor.

'Here's the phone.' She pointed towards the low table in the corner. 'Nick's broken down and the telephone is out of order at the kiosk,' she hurriedly explained to a wide-eyed Melanie.

'When does it ever work?' Melanie sighed. 'Would you like coffee? I'm just making some.' Hardly waiting for Nick's nod of thanks as he held the receiver to his ear, she went back to the kitchen.

'Yes—yes, that's right, at the corner of Wilton Avenue, by a small supermarket.'

'Green's Delicatessen,' Rose whispered in answer to Nick's questioning look.

'You can't get there for at least an hour? OK, thanks anyway. That's right—Nick Coleman. I'm just along the road, but I'll make sure I'm back with the car before you arrive. It's a Ford Granada, pale blue. No, I can't remember the registration number, I'm afraid, it's a hired car.'

He replaced the receiver and turned to face a silent Rose, who sat in the corner of the room, her eyes firmly fixed on the television. The flickering screen cast blue shadows on the ceiling and the characters looked faintly ridiculous with the sound turned down so that the words were indistinguishable.

'Are they able to see to it?' She smiled politely in Nick's direction.

'Yes. The only thing is, they can't get here for about an hour. I'll get along to the pub or something while I'm waiting, to save disturbing you.'

'There's no need for you to leave. We're just having a quiet evening at home, you won't be in the way,' Rose said hastily.

'I find it difficult to believe that you and Melanie

aren't planning an evening out, particularly on a Saturday,' he grinned disarmingly.

He has a lovely smile, Rose thought dreamily, unaware of how closely she was staring. It takes away the rather predatory look, with that strong nose and jawline of his. Unexpectedly sweet.

'Here we are.' Melanie swung back the door, bringing in a waft of freshly brewed coffee and saving Rose from the necessity of a reply for the moment.

She knew that her friend's advice was sound; she would have to tell Nick that she had a child. Putting it off was only going to make the situation more and more difficult. But she hadn't plucked up enough courage to do it just yet!

'I wonder if I might use your bathroom.' Nick held his hands in the air. 'As you can see, I'm not really in a fit state to be handling your cups.'

'Of course—I'll take you through.' Rose led the way to their tiny bathroom, trying frantically to remember if she'd left baby clothes airing in there. But the bathroom was mercifully empty, and after showing Nick the way she handed him a clean towel and returned to the sitting-room.

'Now's your chance. Bring it up in conversation,' Melanie said firmly. 'You don't want to blurt it out like some intense confession.'

'I'll do it—you're right,' Rose agreed. 'But just look at that!' She held shaking hands in the air in a parody of Nick's recent move, but hers were trembling like a leaf about to fall from a tree.

'No excuses, mind. I'll nip out and get the video, give you a chance,' said Melanie.

'Right.' Rose nodded firmly, her thick red-gold hair moving in a sweep about her face, her grey eyes dilated with apprehension.

'That's much more civilised.' Nick appeared in the doorway. 'It's a very nice flat, isn't it? And so much bigger than you'd think from looking at the front of the house. Have you been here long?' He looked appreciatively at the pictures that brightened the far wall from where he was standing, and gazed intently at the display of framed photographs set out on an old-fashioned but highly polished table in the corner.

'It's actually Rose's flat. I'm only the lodger.' Melanie threw a casual jacket around her shoulders and picked up her bag. 'If you'll excuse me, I was on my way to get a film from the video shop. Won't be long.'

The front door closed firmly behind her, the noise a dull echo in the sitting-room.

'Are you sure I'm not spoiling your evening?' Nick gazed intently at Rose as he took the coffee from her with a murmur of thanks.

'For goodness' sake!' she said sharply, her strung-out nerves scarcely able to cope. 'Please don't be so apologetic. You never used to. . . .' She broke off abruptly. 'I'm sorry, I'm rather tired. I don't usually snap at people like that.'

She stirred busily at her cup, not daring to meet Nick's eyes. She'd nearly said too much, had nearly betrayed the fact that she had known him before. Hastily she swallowed her coffee, wishing for a moment it was a glass of brandy. If ever she'd needed Dutch courage! she thought.

'What were you about to say just then?' Nick said slowly.

Impatiently Rose leaned down and flicked off the switch of the television set, then taking a deep breath, dared to look at him.

'I can't remember. I was just rambling, I expect.'

'Rose, please don't lie.' His tone was ominous. 'I'm sure I heard you say that I never used to. . . Never used to what, exactly? What is it you're trying to hide?'

'Truly, it was nothing.' Rose swallowed nervously. 'I was muddling you with someone else. More coffee?' She seized his cup and refilled it, passing the milk jug into his outstretched hand before sitting as far away as possible in the limited space of the room.

'Well,' he sighed, 'I can't force you. You obviously haven't any wish to tell me. And I've no right to press the matter.' He leaned back, his profile thoughtful in the fading light of the room, and there was silence for a moment.

'Your friend is taking a long time. Is it far to the video shop?' He stretched out long legs in front of him, the denim material of his jeans moulded to his powerful thighs, and Rose felt a flutter of desire run through her body, bringing with it a flood of warmth to her face. The sharp lemon tang of his aftershave filled her nostrils, making her almost giddy with her awareness of him. Thankful for the dim light in the room, she looked quickly away as she muttered, 'Not really.'

Without warning, Nick got to his feet, suddenly overpowering as he stood over her. 'Why didn't I think of this before? As soon as the car is fixed, I'll take you and Melanie for a drink to say thank you for putting up with me.'

This is your chance, Rose thought, her heart tripping like a hammer in her chest.

'I can't leave the flat, I'm afraid.' Bravely she stared back at him.

'Oh, sorry. I thought you said you had nothing arranged.' At any other time, his look of disappointment as he sat back on the settee would have warmed her, but not now.

'I would have to organise a babysitter,' she whispered.

'A babysitter?' Nick echoed, his eyebrows raised in a caricature of surprise.

'That's right—a babysitter for my son. And I try not to ask Melanie to sit in the evening, as she looks after him such a lot when I'm working.' The words came out in a scramble, so that by the end of the sentence they had merged into one confused whole.

'Your son?' For a moment Nick didn't say any more. 'I didn't know you had a child. How old is he?'

'Three and a half months.'

His lips tightened in a narrow line. 'Why on earth didn't you tell me before? I thought—I hoped—we were friends.'

'I—er—I—er. . .' she stammered.

'And what about the father? You're not married as well, are you? Another little secret tucked away, perhaps?'

'Of course not! I told you I hadn't any commitments.'

'Well, I would have thought the father of your child was a commitment of some sort, surely?'

'That relationship is in the past. Timmy is mine,' Rose answered fiercely, 'and the fact that he hasn't a father hasn't been in any way a problem.' Up to now, she thought, but that's all changed. What a problem, now that his father's appeared on the scene.

'Here we are—sorry to have been so long.' Melanie's cheery voice cut into the tension in the room as she appeared from the front door, triumphantly carrying two video films aloft. 'I think the whole area must be staying at home tonight to watch videos. The queue was enormous!'

Apparently oblivious of the atmosphere, which to Rose's overstretched nerves was strong enough to cut with the proverbial knife, Melanie draped her jacket over a chair and sat back on the settee beside Nick.

'I wasn't sure if you were going to be staying long,' she smiled in his direction, 'so I thought I'd better not get a sloppy romance, which is what we were thinking of earlier, weren't we, Rose? I hope you haven't seen this.'

'Nick kindly asked us out for a drink,' Rose cut in, carefully dropping the words one by one, like pebbles into water. 'I explained that it would be impossible for me as I haven't a babysitter.'

Melanie nodded, fanning her face with her hand. 'Mmm, it would be awkward. Never mind, we can all cuddle up on the settee and shiver together.'

'You haven't got a horror?' Despite feeling so fraught, Rose couldn't prevent a giggle at her friend's expression, turning involuntarily to catch Nick's eye. Then her laughter died in her throat as she saw the way he was looking at her.

'Is there something wrong?' she faltered.

'No.' He rubbed his hand across his forehead, exploring the silver scar as though it was fresh. 'I was just reminded of something for a moment, but it's gone again.' He shook his head slightly, then took a deep breath. 'If I could use the phone I'll just see if the garage is on the way for my car and leave you both to your horror viewing.'

'Aren't you going to join us?' Melanie looked up from the recorder, as she knelt in front of it.

'Thank you, but I'm not really in the mood.' He twisted his face in a travesty of a smile. 'I'm not very keen on horror films, to tell you the truth. I saw too many unfortunate sights which were real, when I was working in Africa.'

He picked up the phone and quickly pressed the digits on its face, then spoke quietly.

'What happened?' Melanie mouthed behind his back.

'Tell you in a minute,' Rose whispered softly, rubbing at her stomach to try and control the nausea that was cramping her middle.

There was a ting from the corner of the room as Nick replaced the telephone before moving towards the door. 'They should be with me shortly, so I'll go and wait in the car. Thanks again for the coffee. It's nice to have met you.' He bent towards Melanie, still crouched on the floor, and shook her hand.

'I'll see you to the door.' Swiftly Rose got to her feet and hurried into their tiny hall, now almost completely dark.

'Sorry once again to have messed up your evening.' Nick paused by the open front door and looked down at her, his face a white blur, the features indistinguishable in the dim light. The next move sent her rigid with shock.

Bending towards her, he found her mouth with his lips, exploring it gently, then the pressure of his kiss deepened, making every nerve in her body as taut as a violin string. The way his hands encircled her head, his fingers moving through her thick glossy hair, brought remembered sensations thick and fast, so that Rose felt transported into the past.

She steeled herself not to respond, every muscle she possessed frozen, her fists clenched so tightly at her side that her fingernails cut tiny half-moon impressions in the palms. But despite her efforts at control, her body melted in the heat of feelings she'd forgotten she had, as she pressed against Nick's whipcord strength, feeling the length of him moulded into her softness.

'Goodnight, Rose,' he whispered huskily. 'I won't apologise, for I'm not sorry to have done that.' His voice was calm, but as his hand rested for a moment on her shoulder, she felt a tremor run through it, as delicate as the movement of a butterfly's wing, and she could sense the tension in him. 'I don't know. . .' He paused, his eyes dark shadows in the gloom.

'What don't you know?' Rose whispered softly.

'Never mind. It's gone.' He shivered. 'I hope we'll be friends, no further devastating secrets from one another, eh?' Flicking her upturned chin with his finger, he hurried outside, ducking his head slightly as the shadow of a wheeling bat swung out of the bushes by the gate. She watched him set off along the road, his tigerish walk plainly visible in the glow of the neon lights above the shops at the end of the street.

Closing the door behind her, Rose took a deep breath and smoothed an exploratory finger over her mouth, savouring the lingering flavour of Nick's kiss. Then impatiently she shook her head, trying to dislodge the worries that hovered in her brain. What a mess! What a mess! And at the moment she couldn't see any easy way out of it.

CHAPTER FIVE

'I'LL see what I can do, Alan.' Rose moved the telephone to her other hand and perched on the edge of the settee. 'Actually, I may have a daytime babysitter other than Melanie. There's a girl who lives a couple of doors away, she's doing her A-levels and she's used to babies, being the eldest in a big family. I should think she'd be very grateful not only to earn some pocket money, but also to have somewhere quiet to study.'

'Talk about everything happening at once, with Jenny on holiday,' grumbled Alan, his deep voice a murmur down the telephone line. 'I didn't know who else to ask. You're the only one apart from Jenny who has any idea of the running of the office, and won't let everything get in a muddle.'

'When do you have to meet this American travel company?' she asked.

'In a couple of days.'

'And that's in New York? You lucky things!' Rose felt a momentary flicker of envy. She'd always wanted to visit the Big Apple, but hadn't the opportunity as no escort jobs from Fleetline had been sent there.

'That's right. Marjorie has enquired about flights and we could get one the day after tomorrow. If the worst comes to the worst, I'll go on my own. . .'

'There's no need to do that,' Rose cut in quickly. 'I'm sure I'll be able to organise something, and I'll enjoy the change.'

'What about Melanie. . . ?' Alan began.

'Definitely not. She's got a string of early shifts, they're short on the ward, with holidays and so forth. I can't ask her to mess about with the off duty.'

'No, of course not. Well, ring me back. I can arrange to have the phone transferred to you at home for part of the day, but I have to have someone in the office most mornings, at least.'

'How long do you reckon to be away?'

'Four days at the outside. Literally a flying visit.' Alan laughed at his own pun.

'I'll ring you back. Oh, by the way, before you go. How does Nick fit into these arrangements?' Even to say his name made Rose's heart beat faster.

'He's going to be around if there are any problems. It's not awkward for you to work with him, is it?' Alan asked anxiously.

'No, no worries there. Alan,' she added abruptly, 'do you think Nick will ever recover his memory?'

'Rose, my love, I couldn't possibly say. From what I've heard in the past, I would think it must depend on how serious the injury was at the time of the accident, but I've never had much experience in the neurological field. I should think Nick would have seen all the experts, anyway.'

'Of course he would. Silly of me not to think of that. Well, bye for now. I'll be in touch.' Rose was quite proud of the nonchalant tone she managed, but once she had rung off she sat back on the settee with a monumental sigh, her thoughts going over the past week, her expression despondent.

But despite her depression she couldn't prevent a little giggle as she thought back to the look on Alan's face when, acting on Melanie's advice, she had told him the full story.

'I know this isn't something you'd make up, but there's no chance of a mistake, is there?' His greying hair standing on end, his broad pleasant face flushed with worry, Alan had stared in amazement when she had explained that Nick was Timmy's father.

'Of course she hasn't made a mistake. Don't talk such rubbish! You can't get in a muddle over something as important as that.' Marjorie had hurried across their large sitting-room and flung her arms around Rose in a fiercely reassuring hug. 'As if you haven't had enough to put up with, thinking Timmy's father was dead, and now there's this. Don't worry, we'll do all we can to help—you know that, don't you?'

Rose had swallowed at the lump in her throat. Marjorie was usually so quiet, preferring to stay in the background, that her burst of emotion had come as a shock to Rose's shattered nerves. But it had been no less a comfort, for all that.

As though her thoughts of her son had reached him, there was a cry from the bedroom and, glad of the interruption to her gloomy frame of mind, Rose hurried to the bedroom and swung Timmy into her arms.

'Honestly, Timmy,' she murmured against his

velvety cheek, 'you seem to grow almost between feeds! I swear you're heavier than you were this time yesterday.' His dark sherry-coloured eyes focused as she spoke, a wide gummy smile bringing a dimple to his cheek. 'Come on, I'll change you, give you a drink, then we'll see if Beverley's at home and would be willing to babysit when I have to work. I must admit——' she placed the baby on his changing mat and peeled his light blue sleep-suit away from his arms and legs '—I would enjoy a few days' work in the office—I quite fancy the power of being in charge!'

Neatly fixing a clean nappy in place, then putting bright red dungarees on Timmy's constantly waving legs, she tossed the dirty clothes into the Ali Baba basket and lifted Timmy, holding him close, delighting in his sweet baby smell. He frowned for a moment as she propped him in the bouncy swing in the kitchen, then decided he was happy after all.

There had been no word from Nick since his unlooked-for visit on the night his car had broken down. Rose wasn't sure whether she was glad or sorry for the respite. In a way it would have been reassuring to see what his attitude was to the knowledge of Timmy, but at the same time she dreaded meeting him again after his unexpected kiss. For it had shown her, as nothing else had, the attraction she still felt, the surge of emotion that had set her body on fire, despite her determined efforts to remain detached.

'Tell you what, Timmy, I wouldn't want to spend too much time alone in your daddy's company. Not because of what he might do, but because of what I might want to do in return.' She glanced out from the kitchen window. The sun still streamed from an impossibly blue sky, the weather set fair for the morning. Taking a bottle of orange juice from the fridge, Rose packed it neatly in her big red carryall, with clean nappy, tissues and an apple and book for herself, then struggled the pushchair from the porch outside the kitchen door, took Timmy from his bouncer and strapped him firmly into place. He lay back contentedly chewing his thumb, tolerating the floppy white sun-hat, that made him look like a tiny cricketer about to leave for the crease.

'A matched pair!' she laughed, glancing down at her own red cotton shorts and T-shirt, then back again at Timmy's dungarees. Levering the pushchair outside, she locked the back door behind her and hurried out through the garden gate, sniffing unconsciously at the strong smell of creosote that was drawn from the fence by the sun's warmth.

To her relief, Beverley was at home.

'I'd love it, Rose. In fact, I'd be pleased to do it for nothing.' Beverley stood by the front door and paused, holding her glasses in the air, her dark curly hair a halo round her head. 'Just listen to that!' she grinned, and Rose smiled in sympathy as the screeches and yells echoed from the house. A small figure darted up and seized Beverley's denim-clad legs, then rushed away before either girl could speak.

'It won't interfere with you looking after your brothers and sisters, will it?' Rose asked anxiously.

'No, Mum will be pleased that I can have somewhere quiet to study.'

'That's great. They'll probably want me at the office from the day after tomorrow. Will that be all right? About half-past eight.'

'Mm, fine. Isn't he getting lovely?' Beverley cooed, then waved a hasty goodbye and disappeared inside the house, in answer to an almighty crash.

Walking swiftly down the path, Rose turned the push chair on its back wheels and strolled towards the park, her sandals slapping an accompaniment on the hot pavement. Dust lifted in the air with each step, the smell combining with the acrid aroma of tar, which lay in dark tacky patches on the road's surface.

'Phew, Timmy, this has got to be the hottest day yet! I'll be glad to get to the park and in the shade of the trees.'

It was only a short walk, but Rose was sticky and uncomfortable by the time she went through the park gates, her usual interest in the dress shops en route completely smothered as the sun burned with an almost brassy light.

'I know it can't be,' she muttered, 'but it feels nearly as bad as when I did my fateful flight.' She leaned forward and tickled Timmy's rounded tummy. 'The flight that led to you being on the scene!'

She sat thankfully on a wooden seat by the lake. A flotilla of ducks perched immobile on the bottle-green water, not moving enough to cause even a ripple on the surface. Usually, at the sight of a visitor, they would paddle eagerly to the edge of the lake, mouths gaping in anticipation of the feast to come. But now few managed even a beady glare in Rose's direction before resting their heads back, their beaks nestled in the sun-streaked feathers above their wings.

'I think it might be a waste of time trying to feed them today, Timmy. Let's give you a drink, then I think we'll just rest here quietly, where at least there's a suggestion of a breeze.'

The leaves of the horse-chestnut tree hung heavy in the still air, but it was true that now and then there was the faintest zephyr against her skin.

Timmy was obviously as thirsty as she was herself, sucking hungrily at his bottle, the orange drink disappearing in a series of glugging noises, which brought a smile to Rose's face.

'Hey, steady on!' she laughed. But Timmy waved a chubby hand before suddenly belching softly and snuggling into instant sleep.

I wish I could do that, thought Rose enviously, peering at the pages of her book through her dark glasses and biting into the crisp creamy flesh of her apple.

Since Nick's return into her life, her nights had seemed long wakeful hours of almost continuous movement, as she struggled to find a way out of the difficulties brought about by his loss of memory. Melanie had brought home various textbooks from the hospital library, in fact Rose had a copy of one in her hand right now which she had had little chance to study.

Was Nick likely to recover his memory? If he didn't, would it harm him to be told the facts about Timmy?

Try as she might, she couldn't seem to take in the meaning of the dry-as-dust prose.

'Post-Traumatic Amnesia. Sometimes patients have islands of memory. . . The length of time of the anmesia can bear relation to the severity. . .' Rose flicked over the pages impatiently. Nothing of what she'd read so far had told her what she wanted to know. '"Sometimes, emotion can play a part in memory loss. . .",' she read aloud. 'I know emotion can play a part, but I don't think they mean the same as me.'

Moodily, she thought back to the visit from Hugh Browne. A tall, lanky man, Melanie's friend from work had tried to explain some of the implications as far as he was able.

'But you have to realise,' he had warned, 'your friend might never fully recover his memory. If the impulses haven't been stored in the part of the brain that deals with long-term memory and have been shunted aside, as it were, while they're still short-term, those impulses could be lost for ever.'

Rose had asked what to her was the most important part of her worry. Would Nick be hurt emotionally if he was told what had gone on during that time?

'It would depend. If he's shut out some of the memories because they were unpleasant, and that can sometimes happen, then it might be harmful. If he's the sort of person to face up to unpleasantness, then there should be no problem.'

With a sigh, Rose dropped the book on to the seat beside her and stared with unfocused eyes at the lake and the sun-drenched ducks. Whatever the outcome, she still was apprehensive at the idea of pushing responsibility on to Nick. He was definitely the sort of person who would accept that he had a moral obligation towards Timmy and herself. She couldn't bear the idea that he might do it only because of a sense of duty.

She retrieved her book and started reading it once more. But soon her eyelids drooped, her head falling back against the surprisingly comfortable rear of the seat. Before long there was a duet of gentle snores coming from mother and son.

It was the feel and sound of drops of water against her bare legs that woke Rose. She sat up with a start, her skin prickling with gooseflesh as the rain fell ever harder. The brilliant sun had gone, swallowed in a grey-bellied sweep of cloud, that was suddenly lit by a streak of lightning. The crack of thunder that followed almost immediately woke Timmy and set Rose's teeth on edge.

The once deserted park was now criss-crossed with hurrying figures paddling helter-skelter through the quickly developing puddles; swearing quietly to herself, Rose spread a waterproof cover over Timmy's ill-clad body and turned towards the gate, nearly losing her sandals in her mad dash for shelter.

She had barely swung the pushchair on to the

pavement when water was thrown up from the gutter over her feet as a large white car pulled up alongside.

'Do you want a lift?' Nick leapt from the driver's seat and seized the handle of the pushchair.

'It's all right,' Rose muttered through chattering teeth, but with a none too gentle sweep of his arm Nick nudged her to one side, lifted Timmy from the chair and pushed them both into the rear seat of the car, before quickly folding the pushchair and putting it in the boot.

Rose sat back with a sigh, clutching Timmy to her middle, his wet legs pressed against her own.

'What a storm!' Slamming the door behind him, Nick settled into the driver's seat and reached across, pulling a large box of tissues from the glove compartment.

'Here, dry what you can of yourself and the baby.'

Wordlessly, Rose took the tissues and began dabbing half-heartedly at Timmy, then at her own face. The last person she wanted to see just now was Nick Coleman, but even her stubborn pride couldn't turn down a haven from the storm, especially for Timmy.

'I haven't seen rain like this since I was in East Africa,' laughed Nick, his face creased in excitement. 'It's exactly like one of those tropical storms that appear literally out of a clear blue sky.' Smoothly he changed gear and peered through the windscreen where the insistent beat of the wipers was almost mesmerising Rose.

'You're not afraid of thunder, I hope?' He glanced through the rear-view mirror at Rose as the car moved with a swish of tyres and quickly covered the short distance to her home.

She shook her head. I'm not afraid of anything except what will happen if you find out about Timmy, she thought, not trusting herself to speak.

'He's a very well behaved baby,' Nick added, pulling up beside the flat. 'Not one peep out of him all the way.'

'It's true, he doesn't cry a lot,' Rose answered, unable to keep a note of pride from her voice.

'You go on and change into some dry clothes. I'll get the pushchair from the boot and bring that in.'

Almost numb with cold, Rose ran up the short path and flung open the front door, Timmy's head bouncing like a flower on a fragile stalk.

'Well, Timmy,' she whispered as she hurried into the bathroom and peeled off his dungarees and hat, 'you don't seem too uncomfortable!' She laughed as Timmy stared back at her with wide dark eyes. 'Which is more than I can say for myself!' She rubbed his small soft body briskly with the towel and wrapped him in a fluffy yellow sleepsuit, before padding in her bare feet to the bedroom to lay him in his cot. There was a murmur of protest, which lasted only a moment, before he found his thumb and settled back into the sleep which had been so rudely disturbed.

'I'm going to take a shower. Help yourself to coffee,' Rose called from the bathroom door, then closed it behind her, not waiting for a reply.

The hot water was comforting and it took only a short time for her to dry herself, spray on a light cologne and slip on her green tracksuit. Tying her hair back from her face, she went shyly to the living-room.

'Do you need to get yourself dry at all, or are you all right?' she asked.

'I'm fine—look, barely damp.' Nick gestured at his dark brown trousers and cream-coloured shirt. 'Here, feel, if you don't believe me.' He leant a shoulder in Rose's direction, grinning as she touched him with the tip of one finger before pulling away.

'I don't bite, you know. Is your. . .' He swallowed. 'Is your son all right? Not too wet?'

Rose shook her head. It was curiously painful to hear him say the words 'your son'. But her face betrayed nothing of what she felt.

'I've made free with the kitchen, found coffee and milk—I hope that's all right.' Nick pushed a mug of coffee towards her and sat back on the settee. 'What were you doing out in such a storm?'

'I'd been to the park,' Rose began. 'Oh, I was supposed to ring Alan. Will you excuse me? He and Marjorie want me to cover for them while they're away, and I said I'd let Alan know.'

Quickly she tapped out the number for the office.

'That's great, Rose—you're a gem! If you could come in for a couple of hours tomorrow, bring Timmy with you if it makes it easier, and I'll go over the relevant bits and pieces. It shouldn't be too difficult, and Nick won't mind if you have to call on him, I'm sure.' Alan cleared his throat, the sound plainly audible in the room. 'Of course, I quite understand that you might want to keep well away from him.'

'I'll see you tomorrow,' Rose interrupted hastily. Talk about Murphy's law! she thought, her face crimson with embarrassment. Normally I have to strain to hear what Alan says, today his voice is as clear as a bell! She looked quickly in Nick's direction. If he'd overheard any of Alan's remarks, he wasn't about to say anything. He sat in his normal relaxed manner, flicking over the pages of the newspaper, sipping at his coffee.

'Everything all right?' He laid the paper down beside him as Rose replaced the receiver, and passed her mug to her.

'Yes, thank you.' She took a mouthful of coffee, peering at him over the rim of her cup. 'I don't know if you heard Alan, but I'm going to the office tomorrow to sort out details of the work, and he offered me your services if I got stuck. I hope that's all right?' She held her breath as she waited for Nick's reply. What would he think if he had in fact heard the remark about it being difficult for her to work with him?

'Fine by me. In fact, I'm fairly free over the next few days. I'll come to the office with you tomorrow, if you like, and we can go through it together.'

'OK,' nodded Rose. Perhaps he hadn't heard what was said after all. She sighed, thankful that another possibly embarrassing situation hadn't developed. It was going to be difficult enough to cope with his constant company, without looking for undercurrents as well.

They sat not speaking for a moment, the only noise in the room a machine-gun rattle from the storm, as the drops hurled themselves against the window. Rose looked out at the tempestuous weather and shivered, the torrential rain an apt accompaniment to her mood.

'More coffee?' Unable to stand the silence any longer, she got to her feet.

'Rose, sit down,' ordered Nick.

'Eh?'

'Please, sit down. I want to talk to you.'

'What about?' stammered Rose, sinking back into her armchair.

Nick didn't answer immediately, but sat pulling at the hem of his sock as he leaned back, an ankle resting on the opposite knee.

'The other evening, when I called in unexpectedly,' he began quietly, 'I had—well, quite a shock when you told me that you had—that you have, I should say—a child. Don't get me wrong,' he held up an admonitory hand as she opened her mouth to speak. 'I wasn't shocked that you're not married, *per se*. After all, your circumstances are nothing to do with me. But I was hurt, I suppose, that you hadn't mentioned to me before something that's obviously a vital part of your life.'

'But. . .' she began.

'Please, let me finish. I know we haven't known each other very long, but time doesn't always matter in relationships. I felt that there was an affinity between us, and I was under the impression that you felt the same way. And to discover, after several weeks of knowing you, that you'd told me nothing about—Timmy, is he called?'

Rose nodded.

'It was, to put it mildly, a little strange. That's partly the reason for the goodnight kiss.' A smile crossed his face, lifting the shadows that creased his forehead. 'A sort of test, would you call it? I felt the situation was out of my control, and I hate that feeling. I hope it didn't offend you.'

'No. Surprised me, perhaps, not offended,' Rose gulped, as she wondered where the conversation was leading.

'That's good. Now I'll tell you what we're going to do.' Nick stretched across the narrow gap between them and took her hand. 'We're going to start again from scratch. You must know that I'm attracted to you.' He stared deeply into her eyes, his own pools of sherry-coloured darkness. 'And I get the impression that you aren't averse to me. So we'll have no secrets; let's get to know one another, behaving as if we'd just met.' He looked down at her hand as it lay inert in his own, then gently moved his thumb across her palm. 'How do you feel about that idea?'

No secrets, thought Rose. No secrets. I'd love to be able to do what you want, but. . .

'I think it's a very good idea in principle.' She tried to free her hand from his, for the gentle caress sent sensations through her that were hard to control. But he gripped her more firmly.

'But?' he said, his eyebrows raised in a question.

'But sometimes it isn't always possible. . . Oh,

there's Timmy.' With a sigh of relief, she pulled away and hurried from the room.

'Timmy, you angel!' she murmured. 'Talk about saved by the bell. . . Oh!' Her voice lifted in a squeal of protest. 'I didn't realise you'd followed me. You could give a girl a heart attack, creeping up on her like that!'

She cuddled Timmy close to her chest, desperately trying to conceal the tiny features that were an exact copy of the man standing beside her.

'Sorry, I didn't mean to frighten you,' Nick said softly. 'I just came in to see this son of yours properly. You don't mind, do you?'

CHAPTER SIX

'ARE you sure you're quite happy with the schedules? As you can see, we have a doctor escort going out to Paris Thursday, pick up and transfer to Chicago. That's to collect a man who had a heart attack three days ago, and they particularly asked for medical cover. He's had several infarctions in the past.'

Rose sat back in the large leather chair in Alan's office and glanced at the white plastic noticeboard with its few names written in blue waxed crayon. At the moment, it didn't look as though the next few days would be too busy, if the list covered all the bookings to be dealt with.

She turned to Alan. 'Where's the off-duty sheet?' nodding her thanks as he opened the top drawer of the desk and pulled out a red-bound notebook.

'This is a complete list of everyone available. We're a bit short today, but that shouldn't be a problem. I've got two local trips booked for tomorrow; a transfer from the private wing at the General to go to the radiotherapy centre and a man with a fractured femur, who's to have a pin and plate fitted. They want him taken from the geriatric hospital to the orthopaedic theatre.'

Rose stared intently round the small office. It was some time since she had actually been to what was the hub of Alan's ambulance company, and she looked with interest, noting the many small changes. There was now a fax machine and a copier, which certainly hadn't been there before, and a tape recorder by the phone.

Following her gaze with his own, Alan pointed to the small machine.

'I've started to record all booking requests. It gives us a reference in case there's any problem with the patient.' He leant forward and ruffled her hair. 'You know what some of these foreign calls can be like, how they forget to tell us that a patient has a tracheostomy or suffers from asthma when nervous and is terrified of flying.'

He laughed at the horrified look on Rose's face. 'You were the escort nurse that time, weren't you?'

'Yes, I was.' Rose shivered dramatically. 'I thought — Mrs King, wasn't she called? — was going to black out in front of my eyes. She puffed at her inhaler so hard, it was a wonder it didn't disappear down her throat! And when it was time for the plane to land, of course it was a really cloudy day, so the descent was as bumpy as could be.'

'Well, let's hope you won't have anything like that to worry about.' Alan picked up a black flex, complete with plug. 'This is the socket, connect it as soon as someone starts giving details of diagnosis. Other than that, I don't think there's much different from when you were in the office, before Timmy was born.' He bent low and muttered the next few words in a confidential murmur, though they were the only ones present.

'Has Nick shown any signs of recognising you, or remembering what happened?'

Rose shook her head, her thick red-gold hair swinging like a curtain around her face.

'There's been no indication of. . .' She broke off abruptly. 'I wonder if I should say something to him — what do you think?'

'Leave it a bit longer. After all, it's only been a few weeks since he came back into your life.' Alan straightened and stared at the big old-fashioned railway clock, whose sonorous tick was as much a part of the office as any of the newer equipment. 'I must dash. Marjorie will be calling me all sorts of names.'

'Good lord, look at the time!' Rose muttered sympathetically. 'Go on, I'll be fine. Enjoy your stay in New York, the pair of you, and try not to get too bogged down with work. You both deserve a break.'

Alan grinned as he hurried through the door and out into the July sunshine, his lightweight jacket fitting tightly across his broad shoulders.

Rose waved, but he didn't look back, and she sighed as she picked up the small heap of papers from the in-tray and spread them in front of her on the desk.

There seemed to be more work outstanding than she'd at first thought; perhaps she'd been a bit hasty in offering to stand in for Alan and Marjorie. But she stifled her momentary doubts and sorted the sheets into order, placing the ones that looked as though they needed her immediate attention at the top. 'I'll cope,' she told herself firmly, 'and I can always ask Nick if I have any doubts.'

Though after our last meeting, she thought, I'd just as soon not see too much of Nick Coleman just for the present.

She cast her mind back to the afternoon of the storm. She had been unable to think of any good reason not to let Nick take Timmy from her arms, and all the time he'd held her baby son, their baby son, she had been as jumpy as a pea on a drum, to quote one of her father's favourite sayings, waiting for some sign of recognition to cross Nick's face.

She'd had to swallow at a lump in her throat as she'd studied them, for he had been so at ease carrying the baby through to the sitting-room, she'd had to look away in case her expression betrayed some of her thoughts. With a muttered excuse she had hurried to the kitchen and made another tray of coffee.

It wasn't only the cold from her soaking in the rain that had made her splash a generous measure of brandy into both cups; the nervous beating of her heart as she and Nick rested side by side needed something to calm it down. They'd sat without speaking, drinking their coffees and watching Timmy kick and wave his arms, every smile and expression of determination that crossed his face, to her anxious eyes, a facsimile of the man sitting next to her.

Now Rose gazed from the window, not noticing the pedestrians hurrying in the street outside, despite the warmth of the day's sunshine that was rapidly turning the pavements into slabs of heat.

Fumes from the traffic crept through the open window, lightened occasionally by the smell of roasting coffee that made her stomach growl with hunger. But she saw little of the people going about their business. She was still absorbed in wondering about Nick.

Despite Alan's advice, she didn't feel she could carry on much longer without telling Nick the facts of their previous relationship. She'd managed, by dint of great will-power, to keep things on a friendly footing, but she knew that sooner or later her eager heart would betray her and words that she was unable to control would spill from her lips.

And if he was horrified at the truth when he heard it, the heartache she had already suffered would be as nothing compared to the pain she would feel then. It was all very well for him to suggest that they behave as though they'd just met. It should be easy for him. As far as he was concerned, they were relatively new acquaintances, despite the attraction that seemed to be building between them. But she was still full of memories of their past, and it was almost impossible at times not to betray the fact.

As though her thoughts had conjured him out of the air, he appeared at the end of the small shopping precinct. His rangy walk propelled him smoothly through the crowds of shoppers and he seemed to progress without effort, his shoulders in a tan shirt, though trim, looking as strong as ever.

Greedily, she stared, noting the pantherlike walk,

the smooth yet masculine grace, that concealed Nick's amazing strength. She thought back to an occasion in Africa when the worn-out vehicle had finally given up during their trek and remembered the effortless way he had carried Jacinta for nearly five miles. She stifled the memory of her jealousy when his arms had enfolded the injured girl, still ashamed of the feelings she had experienced then.

But there was no time now for dreamy memories. Hastily Rose scrabbled the papers into line, and to her relief, as the door swung back to admit Nick's dark shining head as he peered through the opening, the telephone rang. Her nervous fluster as she tried to connect the recorder lead to the phone was a perfect excuse for the agitation she knew she must be showing, and she managed a friendly grin, only moving away slightly as he came towards her and perched on the arm of her chair.

'Yes, that's right.' She nodded in answer to the telephone enquiry. 'We're more than happy to arrange a road ambulance for your patient, from whatever is the nearest airport to his home, if you'd like us to.'

She smiled over the edge of the receiver as the voice squawked on, trying to keep her eyes averted from the powerful thighs that were close enough to brush against her arm as Nick moved restlessly on the edge of the big office chair.

'The cost. . .? Of course, that would depend on the actual distance and if the patient would need a nurse to travel with him. . . Yes, it works out at about. . .' Hastily Rose picked up the price list from the file.

But Nick got there before her, and their hands met as they both seized the relevant piece of paper.

Rose snatched her hand away, worried that the tremor travelling through her treacherous body at his touch might be obvious to him. But just then a gust of wind blew through the open window, lifting several sheets and scattering them on the floor. In the general scramble to pick them up, the dangerous moment had passed.

'If you'd like to think it over,' Rose said finally, 'and get back to us. . . Of course, any time. Glad to be of help.'

She replaced the receiver and, for the first time since he had come into the office, looked directly at Nick.

Her heart lurched at the way he was studying her.

'Is there anything wrong?' she stammered, pushing a strand of hair behind her ear and tucking her crisp white blouse more comfortably into the waistband of her denim skirt.

'No, of course not.' He shrugged and stood up, prowling round the office, picking up files and replacing them, flicking the pages of a card index, tapping gently at the typewriter keys with his forefinger. 'Are you quite happy about coping with the office?' he asked.

'Yes, I'm fine.' Puzzled at the question, Rose stared at his back, a sudden longing to reach across and smooth her hands over his shoulders almost overwhelming her.

'Is that why you've come in this morning? To check up on me?' Was that the reason for his visit? she thought, swallowing hard at the disappointment that filled her throat. To make sure that there were no problems with the work, not because he wanted to see her? Perhaps he was regretting his suggestion at the flat, that they start again from the beginning in getting to know one another. Unable to stop herself, she snapped out the next few words.

'I worked here before I had Timmy, so I'm pretty used to the routine. That's why Alan and Marjorie were happy to ask me to do the job. But if you've got doubts. . .' Her voice trailed away.

'Of course I haven't got doubts about your *work*.' The emphasis on the last word made her draw her head back nervously as Nick moved towards the desk and leant across, resting both hands on a stack of maps that slithered slowly to the floor. But Rose barely noticed, her eyes drawn to his, gazing into the brandy-coloured depths to try and read what he was thinking.

Every one of her senses was acutely aware of him. She heard the soft sussuration of his breath, smelt a drift of lemony aftershave and drew in the essence of the man. His hand reached and took hold of her nerveless fingers, and she watched almost dispassionately as the fine golden hairs on her forearms stirred with an independent life of their own.

'The only doubts I have,' Nick whispered huskily, 'are. . . Blast!' he added as the telephone rang shrilly, its jangling note piercing the tension that filled the room.

Whatever his doubts were, Rose didn't have the chance to discover, for thereafter the calls came thick and fast and she barely had time to drink the coffee that Nick thoughtfully poured for her, as she answered queries, took bookings for ambulances and also arranged for one of their nurses to travel by scheduled flight to Alicante to collect an elderly gentleman who had fallen and broken his wrist.

'Do you need an escort nurse for that?' Rose demurred.

'He has a right-sided weakness from a previous stroke, and his wife is frail.' The Spanish accent of the insurance agent made the details a little difficult to follow, but once Rose had noted everything, carefully recording what was said as a safeguard against mistakes, the flights were arranged and she had organised a nurse to fly out that evening.

Twice Nick attempted to continue what he had started to say, but by the time the fourth call cut in he had obviously had enough. He patted Rose on the arm, mouthed a goodbye and went through the door to the street outside.

Anxiously looking from the window, Rose watched as he scuffed impatiently at a small stone on the pavement edge, before turning on his heel and walking away, his shoulders hunched in a caricature of bad temper.

'It's not my fault that it's been busy,' she murmured grumpily to the empty room. And she could barely control her irritation as the time went on and the telephone stayed annoyingly silent once he had left. She found herself obsessed with wondering what Nick had been about to ask. Did he have a glimmering of memory? Was he going to ask her more about Timmy? Perhaps he would. . .?

'I must concentrate,' she told herself sternly as she found several files in the wrong order and realised she hadn't put the latest bookings on the noticeboard.

Completing the few details remaining, she flicked on the switch of the answerphone, picked up her bag and hurried from the office, locking the heavy wooden door behind her. In her early morning rush, she had eaten very little breakfast. Maybe if she had something now, she might feel a little brighter.

The coffee house, its dark green front open wide to let in the warm summer air, had always served excellent snack lunches in the past.

A salad, some crusty bread and even a piece of their dark chocolate cake would help her through the afternoon; at the moment, the prospect of another three or four hours in the office was daunting, and she definitely deserved a break, she thought emphatically. And there was nothing to beat a wodge of gooey carbohydrate to lift the spirits, even if it did add inches to her waistline.

'*Blast*!' Impatiently Rose scrubbed at the speck of chocolate sauce on the snowy-white front of her blouse. It was no good; try as she might, she couldn't shift the mark. She threw the napkin down beside her empty plate and took her purse from her bag. There was no time to stop for coffee, for the little restaurant had been particularly busy and she had waited some time to be served.

'Could I. . .?' She waved her hand in the air in an attempt to catch the waitress's eye, but the girl either didn't or wouldn't see her.

'Do you mind if I sit here with you?' Startled, Rose looked up at the familiar outline of the tall figure by the table. Nick's features were unreadable as he stood with his back to the golden sunshine that spread like melted butter across the front of the shop.

'Of course I don't.' She shifted uncomfortably in her seat. 'But I'm afraid I was just leaving. I'm waiting for the girl to bring my bill.'

'Is there any reason to rush away?' He leant back in his chair and picked up the menu card. 'I was hoping you might stay and keep me company. I assume you've already eaten?'

He seemed to be gazing directly at the chocolate stain on her blouse.

'I should have thought it was fairly obvious,' Rose said more abruptly than she intended, embarrassed at being caught at a disadvantage. 'How did you know I'd be here, anyway?'

'Just an inspired guess.' Nick grinned, his teeth a flash of white. 'The office was empty, the answerphone switched on, and I knew you wouldn't want to go too far.' He paused and stared around the busy restaurant, mostly filled with women shoppers, their summer dresses splashes of colour like flowers in a garden. 'It's very pleasant, isn't it? And nice and cool.'

The door stood wide, the sun gilding the polished wooden floor and tables. Crisp white napkins and shining cutlery lent a sparkle that made everything look almost indecently clean. Drifting from the kitchen at the rear came the occasional waft of hot bread.

'I've always enjoyed their food,' Rose agreed. 'I used to come here when I worked in the office before. They were always very nice to me when I was expecting Timmy, found me a comfortable table, usually in the corner out of the way.' She smiled in memory. 'One day I made a pig of myself with some pistachio ice cream. I had terrible indigestion and I'm sure the staff all thought I was about to go into labour! Talk about panic!'

'I can't understand the man.' Nick cut abruptly into her reminiscences.

'Pardon? What man?' Rose stared back blankly. But Nick was unable to answer immediately, for just then the waitress hurried across.

'Mmm—chicken salad and a mineral water, please.' He threw the card back on to the table and turned to look at Rose once more. Again his face was in shadow, making it difficult for her to read his expression.

'Er—you started to say something just now, Nick.'

'Oh, yes. In fact, it's part of what I was trying to say to you earlier, back in the office, but couldn't because of all the interruptions.'

Rose glanced at her watch, but the tiny figures

were difficult to see, and when she looked up Nick was frowning thoughtfully.

'My father gave me this when Timmy was born, but I can hardly see the time on it, the. . .' Her voice trailed off as he leant across the table and stared into her eyes.

'I can't understand why Timmy's father isn't fighting tooth and nail to get you to go back to him. He isn't, is he?'

Rose stared back open-mouthed.

'He — er — he — er. . .' she stammered, conscious of the wave of colour that swept over her face. How was she supposed to answer such a question? She'd been afraid of the possibility of the subject cropping up, for several times Nick had led the conversation round to Timmy's father.

But now, asking her out of the blue had knocked her sideways. She felt almost as though she'd been given a physical blow, her stomach cramping suddenly against the meal she'd eaten, her heart beating so loudly she thought it must be audible to Nick on the opposite side of the table.

She was saved from replying by the arrival of the waitress. Seizing the opportunity to collect her bill as the plate of salad was placed in front of Nick, she pushed back her chair, scraping the legs along the polished floor.

'I think I'd better get back, Nick, if you'll excuse me. The answerphone must be almost burning up with overload.'

'You obviously still care for him.' Nick pushed a piece of lettuce across his plate, his head bent

GET 4 BOOKS A CUDDLY TEDDY AND A MYSTERY GIFT

Return this card, and we'll send you 4 Mills & Boon Romances, absolutely FREE! We'll even pay the postage and packing for you!

We're making you this offer to introduce you to the benefits of Mills & Boon Reader Service: free home delivery of brand-new Romance novels, at least a month before they're available in the shops, FREE gifts and a monthly Newsletter packed with offers and information.

Accepting these 4 free books places you under no obligation to buy, you may cancel at any time, even just after receiving your free shipment.

Yes, please send me 4 free Mills & Boon Romances, a Cuddly Teddy and a Mystery Gift as explained above. Please also reserve a Reader Service Subscription for me. If I decide to subscribe, I shall receive six superb new titles every month for just £10.20 postage & packing free. If I decide not to subscribe I shall write to you within 10 days. The free books and gifts will be mine to keep in any case. I understand that I am under no obligation whatsoever. I may cancel or suspend my subscription at any time simply by writing to you.

Ms/Mrs/Miss/Mr _____ 4A3R

Address _____

_____

_____ Postcode_____

Signature_____
I am over 18 years of age.

Get 4 Books a Cuddly Teddy and Mystery Gift FREE!

SEE BACK OF CARD FOR DETAILS

Mills & Boon Reader Service,
FREEPOST
P.O. Box 236
Croydon
CR9 9EL

Offer expires 31st August 1993. One per household. The right is reserved to refuse an application and change the terms of this offer. Offer applies to U.K. and Eire only. Readers overseas please send for details. Southern Africa write to: Book Services International Ltd., P.O. Box 41654 Craighall, Transvaal 2024. You may be mailed with offers from other reputable companies as a result of this application.
If you would prefer not to share these opportunities, please tick this box. ☐

No stamp needed

forward, the dark swathe of his hair shielding his eyes. 'You'll do anything rather than talk about him.' He sounded so dejected, Rose felt her inner self curl in sympathy. At the same time, she knew a sudden lift of spirits, for surely Nick's dejection must mean that he had a genuine interest in what was happening to herself and Timmy.

'Nick, please believe me. When I can tell you the circumstances of Timmy's background, I will, I promise.' Clear grey eyes stared into brown and she drew in a deep breath, scarcely daring to believe what she thought she could read in Nick's expression. Giving a slight cough, she squeezed his hand with her own long fingers.

'I know you will.' He gazed back at her. 'I don't usually feel sorry for myself, but sometimes I get so frustrated at not being able to remember, and then when there seems to be another mystery. . .' He took his hand from her grasp and pushed it impatiently through his hair. 'Anyway, I'll call in at the office as soon as I've finished eating.' His smile was strained, but at least it was a smile, thought Rose, as she hurried out into the brilliant afternoon sun and walked the few yards to the door of the office.

The light from the telephone was flashing as she went up to the desk, so, turning off the answerphone, she picked up the receiver.

'Hello, is that Rose?' For a moment Rose didn't recognise the soft breathy tones.

'Beverley? What's wrong? Has something happened to Timmy?' Her voice sharpened anxiously.

'No, of course not. Just to tell you that I'm taking him to the park this afternoon as it's such a lovely day. Is that all right?'

Rose slumped down into the chair. 'Of course it is. You know where all his clean clothes are, don't you?'

'Yes, I've got everything under control.' Sounding far more mature than her seventeen years, Beverley then spoilt the image with a giggle. 'I think there might be a surprise for you when you get home. What time will that be?'

'I'll get everything sorted here and probably leave about four. What's the surprise?'

'If I tell you it won't be a surprise,' Beverley countered in reasonable tones.

'Is it nice or nasty?' Rose asked sharply.

'Nice, of course. I'll see you later.'

Rose took a deep breath and replaced the receiver. 'I'm as jumpy as can be,' she told the empty room as she rewound the messages on the tape and stretched out in the chair, putting her sandalled feet on the edge of the desk. 'It doesn't help having Nick hovering, much as I love to be with him.'

There were only two messages which rattled noisily in her ear, and she noted the numbers, then went to the kettle in the corner of the room, filled it and switched it on. Really it was too hot for coffee, but she needed something to get her brain into gear. Dabbing again at the mark on her blouse, she didn't notice the door swing back, and jumped nervously as Nick spoke.

'Can I help you with any of the calls?'

He stood beside her, his gaze fixed on the open window. His manner was cool, his speech crisp and businesslike.

'No, thank you. There isn't anything I can't deal with.' Rose made sure her manner was as formal. 'I was just about to make a coffee. Would you like one?'

'No, I must get on. There's someone I have to see.' He moved towards the door.

'But I thought you were going to. . .' Rose bit her lip, trying to disguise her disappointment.

'Well, I've changed my mind.' He smiled at her and gently flicked her cheek with his finger. 'Don't say you'll miss me. I'm flattered! I'll phone or see you before you leave. What time do you hope to get away?'

'About four.'

'If it's awkward for you to have the line transferred to your number later, let me know and I'll take any calls. I should be back by five.' He dropped a friendly kiss on her upturned face and hurried from the office.

Well, that's a sudden change, thought Rose grouchily. She wouldn't admit, even to herself, that although she'd been dreading having Nick in the office when he mentioned it earlier, now that he'd left and in rather a hurry, a contrary feeling of discontent made her frown heavily as she poured a solitary cup of coffee and plodded towards the desk.

She hurriedly placed the cup on the desk as the telephone's shrill summons broke into her thoughts.

'Sorry, could you speak up?' Edging round the desk, Rose perched on the large office chair and pulled a sheet of paper towards her. 'You need someone this afternoon? What, more or less straight away? Doctor and nurse? Corfu? Head injury? Give me your number and I'll get back to you as quickly as I can.'

Hastily replacing the receiver, she took the on-call duty roster from the drawer. Only two possible nurses, she saw, staring at the names anxiously.

And her anxiety was justified, for one staff nurse was out, and the other had no experience of head injuries.

I suppose I could go —— Rose tapped thoughtfully at her teeth with a pencil, the staccato rhythm almost an echo of her heartbeat. But she couldn't ring Beverley to tell her, she'd taken Timmy to the park.

Taking a deep breath, she picked up the receiver once more, ran her finger down the list of numbers on the telephone pad and tapped the sequence written there.

'Nick, I need a doctor and nurse urgently for a flight. At the moment I can't get a nurse to cover and I'm trying to arrange to go myself.'

His voice unusually tinny over the car phone, Nick abruptly snapped the question at her.

'What's the matter with the patient?'

'A little boy, knocked down, in Corfu. Head injury, and from the preliminary report it sounds as though it could be quite serious. I know from previous trips that there aren't CAT scan facilities on the island. The insurance company doctor wondered if it might be more straightforward for us to fetch him and bring him back to the UK.'

'Certainly much better,' he agreed. 'I'm on my way back to the office. Get on to the air ambulance; if we're lucky, we could be out of Gatwick within a couple of hours. Did they give you any details about his neurological state?'

'Not too many. Unconscious, some response to painful stimuli, but that's all I stopped to ask about.'

'Right, you know what to do. It will almost certainly be as easy to get him back here as to attempt a transfer to Athens.'

With an abrupt goodbye, Rose replaced the receiver, picked it up again and dialled the booking office of the air ambulance company. There was an executive jet available, it could be ready for take-off in a couple of hours.

Quickly she made the booking, then dialled her home number.

As she thought, no reply.

But her next call was successful.

'Melanie, I've got to go to Corfu, there's a head injury that needs to be brought back to the UK urgently and I can't get hold of Beverley. Will you be at home this evening?'

'Sure, don't worry about it. I'll take care of Timmy. What time are you leaving?'

'In about two hours, I hope. Nick's coming back to the office, and I'd think the best bet would be for us to go straight to Gatwick. There's a spare uniform here I can use.'

'Nick, eh?' Melanie said knowingly.

'Oh, Melanie, I wish I could get things sorted out with him. It's just so unfair, like living in limbo,' Rose groaned. 'I just can't seem to decide how much to tell him, if anything at all, and every time I pluck up the courage to say something I get cold feet.'

'Well, perhaps you can find a way to straighten things out when you get back. Don't do anything I wouldn't do while you're away, mind.'

'Chance would be a fine thing! We'll be too busy for hanky-panky.'

'What a funny old-fashioned word!' Both girls were giggling as they said goodbye.

Hanky-panky! Rose snorted to herself, but then had to hurry to arrange a transfer of the telephone for the time of her absence.

Luckily Ron, one of the paramedics, was happy to take the line. It was only a few minutes' work for Rose to ring through to the insurers in Corfu, change into a white tunic and navy trousers, then to sit back and wait impatiently for Nick's return. Would they have the opportunity to talk over things, or would she still be in the same situation when she got back? Who could tell?

Sometimes she felt as though she'd been in a state of suspended animation for ever. She shrugged. Whatever the outcome, at least she was able to look forward to spending time with Nick. Even if nothing was resolved, they might become closer friends. And she found the hope was enough to bring an edge of excitement to the forthcoming trip.

CHAPTER SEVEN

ANXIOUSLY Rose stared from the window of the ambulance car, then looked down at her watch pinned to the front of her tunic. The traffic on the roads leading towards Gatwick was getting steadily heavier the nearer they got to the airport, but as she glanced at Nick he smiled reassuringly.

'We'll be there on time—stop fretting! At least we won't have all the waiting in the baggage queues; checking in should be quite straightforward.'

'Yes, but,' Rose began, 'even so, our medical equipment will have to be scanned, and if we miss our take-off slot, with it being the holiday season, it could mean a long wait for another.'

'Do you always get in such a tizzy?' Nick raised his strong dark eyebrows, grinning in sympathy as Rose subconsciously raised her watch and looked at it once more.

'I'm sorry. It's quite a long time since I've done a flight job, because of Timmy, of course, and I can't help feeling nervous in case something delays us.' She paused, biting her lip. 'And the little boy's head injury sounded quite severe.'

'We'll deal with it, never fear. Here we are—Gatwick; now we just have to go to the commercial section and with luck our plane should be ready for us. Did you get a chance to make sure all our kit was up together before we left the office?'

'Of course,' Rose snapped, her nerves as tight as a drum, partly because of the tension of the flight and partly at being thrown so unexpectedly into Nick's company once more. Her earlier feeling of expectancy had disappeared, leaving her edgy and short-tempered.

'OK, don't get huffy!' Nick was silent as he threaded the car through the thinning traffic, past the arrivals area, and into a gateway in a high wire fence, at last reaching the main loading section of the airfield.

'Sorry. Actually, Airport Security is usually very helpful on rush jobs such as this one and will come to the plane if the transit office has organised it,' Rose muttered as they swung past the end of the main runways and pulled up outside the booking office of the executive jet company.

Fleetline owned a small turbo-engine plane which was used for the shorter European flights, but in a job such as the present one, where they would be flying to Corfu, and then were taking the little boy directly to the neurosurgical hospital near his home in Liverpool, the extra mileage available on the jet was essential.

The formalities of loading, security checks and passports were quickly dealt with, and barely two hours after the original phone call they were airborne, turning into the sunlit sky which shone with an iridescent glow that filled the little aircraft with an almost unearthly light.

'Right,' Nick said briskly as the seat-belt light was extinguished, 'let's have a coffee while we run over the details of our patient, as many of them as you've been told, anyway.'

'I'll get the drinks.' Unclipping her belt, Rose moved towards the front of the plane, crouching down beside the small hot-water boiler and setting out cups for herself and Nick. There was no point in asking the pilots if they wanted a drink as yet; they were always too busy just after take-off to bother with anything other than the essentials of the flight.

She was perturbed to see that her hands were shaking slightly as she tore open the small packets of coffee granules and poured them into the cups. Her nerves were worse than she'd thought. Was it the flight, or was it the thought of being to all intents and purposes alone with Nick for at least a couple of hours? Was he likely to try to discuss their relationship again? After all, since that rainy afternoon at the flat, they'd barely seen one another to talk to. And the constant interruptions at the office had stopped any attempt at personal conversation.

Who could tell? In the meantime, she must try and pull herself together, for the job ahead could be tricky and it was some time since she'd done an air ambulance flight.

Still, she muttered to herself, as she moved carefully along the narrow gangway of the plane, balancing the plastic tray and cups uncertainly in front of her, I don't expect I'll have forgotten the routine that much. And I did look after neurosurgical cases when I worked in ITU.

'Thanks.' Nick scooped the cup from the tray and sat back in his seat. 'Now tell me all you can about this patient. I couldn't get hold of the doctor in charge at the other end before we left, so I'll have to rely on your report.' He bent close to her, his breath caressing the edge of her cheek, the clean-cut lemon smell of his aftershave drifting softly into her nostrils. Rose gulped again at her coffee to try and regain her composure, then wished she hadn't, for it was so hot it burnt her tongue.

'Damn!' she exclaimed.

'What?' Nick pretended to look shocked, raising his eyebrows in a caricature of disapproval.

He has the most attractive eyebrows, Rose thought musingly, even as she drew air sharply into her mouth in an attempt to cool the burn.

Heavens, I must be besotted, if I'm swooning over his eyebrows now! she thought. She had to stifle a giggle at the bizarre thought, suddenly aware that Nick was staring at her, a puzzled look on his face.

'Sorry, I was just thinking of something.' Quickly she took out the report and pulled the first sheet from its protective blue plastic cover. 'Jeremy Morgan, ten years old, I think, knocked down by a car when crossing the road. Was conscious on admission to the clinic...'

'What time was this?' Nick interrupted sharply.

'I'm not sure exactly — about lunchtime, I believe.'

'Right, carry on.'

'He'd started to deteriorate and was unresponsive when I last spoke to Corfu. Though again, I'm not sure if that was to painful stimuli, or voice, or what.'

'Could be an extra-dural.' Nick frowned thoughtfully. 'I hope not. And no CAT scan.'

'They've done a skull X-ray, no sign of a fracture, and they were going to give steroids and possibly Mannitol,' Rose told him.

'Well, it's no use worrying until we get there. It might be as well to try and get some sleep.'

'I'm too wound up to sleep,' grumbled Rose. But her mutterings were stifled in a small squeak of protest, for Nick settled himself into the seat beside hers, put his arm around her and pulled her head on to his shoulder.

'Will that help you to relax?'

She stiffened, aware of every detail of his strong muscular body. Far from helping her to relax, his closeness made every nerve she possessed tingle into a life of its own.

Struggling free, she took a book from her flight bag and ostentatiously opened it, gazing at the words on the page as though her life depended on it.

She knew that Nick was watching her, and could sense the mischievous grin that lit his face. But she was determined to appear cool and in control, and after a few moments she felt rather than heard him sigh, and he too picked up a book and appeared as absorbed as she hoped she looked.

But the printed page was unable to hold her attention, and when she realised that she'd read a paragraph three times without taking in one word she shut the book with a slap and stared from the window.

Below them, banks of white fluffy cloud formed a

snow-like scene, occasional air currents sending up peaks like tiny white volcanoes. She saw another plane travelling beneath them, the illusion that it was hardly moving exaggerated in the crystalline air. She felt almost mesmerised as their air ambulance droned on steadily, effortlessly covering the miles to their destination.

'It's amazing, isn't it?' she piped up suddenly. 'All those thousands of people down there, and here we are, floating above their heads like gods. They're completely unaware of us.'

Nick turned towards her and smiled in agreement.

'Mmm,' he murmured. 'It's a bit like seeing into a lighted window. You haven't any idea what the life is of the people inside, they could be unhappy, lonely, ecstatic, contented—who knows? But even though you might not envy them their life, you still feel very much left out.'

'I can't imagine that you'd ever feel left out,' Rose raised her eyebrows. 'You've never told me about your family.' She held her breath, not sure why she waited with such nervous anticipation for Nick's answer. It seemed strange to think that despite their time together in Africa, they had revealed so little of their backgrounds. Somehow it hadn't mattered; all that had been important was the daily struggle to stay ahead of the fighting, to keep their patient as comfortable as possible and to savour the physical closeness that had grown so rapidly between them.

'My parents live in Somerset now,' Nick told her. 'Dad retired early, and they both enjoy village life.'

'And what about your sister?' Rose asked absent-mindedly, remembering that once in the past, Nick had mentioned a younger sister.

He stared at her intently. 'How did you know I had a sister?'

Rose swallowed nervously, abruptly aware of her mistake.

'You mentioned her at some time, I can't remember when it was. It must be nice to have a family,' she added hastily.

Nick was silent for a moment.

'My sister lives with my parents.' He grinned, lost in thought. 'She was the bane of my life when we were younger! She pretends she doesn't like the human race and is an assistant to a vet—much prefers animals. She says she can't understand how I can put up with people, especially when they're ill.'

'That's not very. . .' Rose paused. She didn't want to sound as if she was criticising.

But Nick appeared not to have heard.

'How about your family? You never tell me anything about yourself.'

'My mother's dead, she died when I was seven. Dad works in the Middle East, so I don't see him very often.' She gave an unwitting sigh. 'I suppose Alan and Marjorie are the nearest I have to a family, at home.'

'Apart from Timmy.'

'Of course.' Her face lit up. 'He's the most important aspect of my life, of course. I hope Melanie is taking good care of him.'

'And how about Timmy's father?' Nick asked

softly, gazing ahead towards the front of the plane. But though Rose couldn't see his expression, she could sense a sudden stiffening in his shoulders, and for one brief moment he looked bleak. 'I'm probably poking my nose in where it's not wanted, and I'm sorry. It's only because I like you—like you a lot. And I find it difficult to understand how he can be pushed so completely out of your life. I'm probably treading on dangerous ground, but don't you have any contact with him?'

Hastily Rose stretched up in the seat.

'Would you like more coffee?' she asked.

'No, I wouldn't like more coffee, not until you explain a few things to me.'

'You've got no right——' Her voice faltered. Of course, if truth be told, he did have rights, certainly to get to know Timmy, but in what circumstances? She couldn't, just *couldn't* back him into a corner by explaining. Instinctively she knew he would do what he considered was the correct thing and take responsiblity for the pair of them. And that wasn't what she wanted at all. He had to come to her wholeheartedly, because he wanted to spend his life with her and Timmy, even if he didn't regain his memory. A small groan forced its way from her lips.

'Rose, sit still! I'm not letting you move until you answer me honestly. Are you and Timmy's father likely to get back together?'

'I don't know!' yelled Rose, almost in tears. 'Don't keep on.'

'All right, I won't. But just let me ask you one thing. Do you still love him?'

'Nick... Nick...' Swallowing hard, she stared at him, her distress apparent in every line of her face, her grey eyes almost the colour of indigo as she tried to think of a truthful answer.

'Don't attempt to say any more. It's obvious that you do still care for him, and I have no right to pester you. It's nothing to do with me.' He got up from the seat and moved forward to the cockpit. The whole shape of his back and shoulders looked upset. Rose swore under her breath and once more picked up her book.

Oh, how I wish there was someone I could go to for advice! she thought. Nick turned and stared at her, and for a moment she wondered if she'd spoken the words aloud.

But just then the seatbelt light flashed overhead and Nick perched in the front seat, just behind the pilots and well away from her. They sat apart, neither looking towards nor taking notice of the other.

Rose watched from the window as the plane banked and turned. Soon the lights of the airport on Corfu were shining below them as the plane swept round, the thump of the undercarriage and flaps signifying that they were soon to land.

'Do you speak English?' Rose had to grit her teeth to stop the cry of pain forcing its way from her lips as Jeremy's father seized her arm, almost shaking her in an agony of relief. 'Thank God! I can't understand a word of what's going on!'

He pushed her none too gently towards a narrow

door that led to a small six-bedded ward, his face working nervously.

'I've never known anything so frustrating. . .' His voice trailed away as he stood back to allow Nick and Rose to approach the bedside.

'We'll soon have everything sorted and your boy will be back in your own hospital before you know it.' Warmly Nick shook the hands of the couple, who looked absurdly young, dressed as they both were in brightly coloured beachwear. They huddled together as though trying to draw strength from one another, their hands clasping and unclasping, while they waited for Nick to examine their son. Rose stared down at the little boy.

He seemed overwhelmed in the adult bed, his fair hair plastered to his head, his cheeks stained with flags of red. The sound of his breathing filled the small room, the harsh noise audible above the chattering of the relatives of the other patients.

Gently Nick studied Jeremy, carefully pushing back his almost transparent eyelids, flashing the light from a small pocket torch into the pupils. He lifted arms and legs in turn and let them fall back on to the sheet, then checked the resistance of Jeremy's fingers against the palm of his own hand.

'Will he be all right?' Mrs Morgan, a slim fair-haired woman, hugging her large pale blue shirt more closely round her bikini, stared anxiously at Nick as he carried out the brief examination.

'I can't say exactly how serious the injury is.' Nick moved to stand beside the apprehensive couple, shuffling in the narrow space between the beds.

Rose was unable to hear what he said next. She gazed at the other patients with barely concealed interest, noting the pallor on the face of a man in the corner bed, momentarily surprised as another patient was helped by an elderly grandmother figure in black to get out of bed and walk towards the door.

She turned, and realised that Nick had gone to speak to a white-coated female doctor, whose thick curly hair was clipped back and shone like a cascade of dark silk in the nape of her neck.

Rose moved closer to hear the discussion.

'We have made an X-ray, given steroids—Dexamethasone, I think you call it.' The doctor laughed, a deep gurgling chuckle that seemed out of place in the rather grim surroundings of the ward. 'I'm sorry I do not have good English.'

Nick smiled sympathetically. 'It's a lot better than my Greek! If I could perhaps see the X-ray then we can get our patient away to the airport and home.' They went out through the door together, an easy camaraderie obvious from the way they held their heads close as they spoke, and Rose had to grit her teeth against a wave of physical jealousy that made her senses spin for a moment. Quickly she shook her head as though to clear the unpleasant thoughts that hovered there, and turned, with what she hoped was a reassuring smile, to the waiting parents.

'Are you both coming with us in the air ambulance?' she asked with an attempt at brisk efficiency that she was far from feeling. What on earth were Nick and the lovely Greek doctor discussing so intently in the corridor just outside?

'Our friends are going to take most of our luggage. I've just got a weekend case and clothes more suitable to change into; we'd both like to be with Jeremy, in case. . .' Mrs Morgan's voice faltered and she reached to the bed and took hold of the little boy's hand. He still lay as unmoving as when Nick and Rose had arrived.

'Come on, now.' Pushing aside her own concerns, which seemed so trivial compared with the worries of the people in front of her, Rose put a reassuring arm around the woman's thin shoulders. 'It'll take very little time to get you back to Liverpool. I'm glad you were able to sort out your luggage, as the space on the plane is very limited.'

She moved around the bed. 'Just wait there while I go and see what arrangements have been made so far. I know there's an ambulance already waiting to take us to the airport, and if Dr Coleman is happy for Jeremy to be moved, I think we'll be leaving very soon.'

She went out through the ward door. There was a trolley ready, the two attendants in their white jackets and trousers chatting quietly as they waited. Neither could speak English, but their smiles and gestures were easy to understand and so full of good will that for the first time since their arrival, Rose began to relax. Efficiently they manoeuvred the stretcher alongside the bed and lifted Jeremy gently across, covering him with a folded sheet.

As they went back into the corridor, struggling to get the stretcher through the narrow gangway, Rose caught a glimpse of Nick shaking hands with the

Greek doctor. Was it her imagination, or did the clasp of their hands seem unnecessarily prolonged?

However, she didn't have time to worry now. The most important thing was to make their way through the traffic as quickly as possible and get their little entourage airborne.

Rose glanced at her patient once more. She wouldn't be sorry when the job of transferring him to the care of an expert neurological unit in the UK had been completed. Until then it was her responsibility, with Nick, of course, to make sure that Jeremy's condition didn't deteriorate. And with a determined shrug of her shoulders she pushed aside all thoughts of her own problems and walked towards the lift beside the stretcher.

It was reassuring that it was Nick who was the doctor on the flight. If anyone could cope with unexpected complications, he could. And Rose was relieved to see the friendly grin that crossed his face as he hurriedly followed them, an envelope of X-rays tucked under one arm, his medical bag held tightly in his hand.

'All right?' he grinned at her.

'Fine, thank you.' Conversation was halted as they squeezed into the lift which creaked in an unwilling fashion to the ground floor.

'I shan't be sorry to get to the plane,' Rose murmured softly, leaning close to Nick and acutely aware of the way he was looking at her. She gazed back into the depths of his sherry-coloured eyes, subconsciously noting the strange light in them.

But he blinked and looked abruptly away, turning to the attendant.

'How long to the airport?' He held his arm aloft and pointed to his wrist. 'How long to the airport?'

The man, who had been watching them with unabashed interest, shrugged, then grinned.

'Thirty minute. OK?'

'OK,' nodded Nick. They clanked their way from the lift and through the door to the waiting ambulance.

As they loaded their young patient, Rose's skin prickled. For Nick started to whistle, tunelessly, as he had when they had first met. And the evocative noise sent her mind scurrying back. Would he ever remember? she thought, as she scrambled into the rear of the vehicle beside her unconscious patient. If he didn't, she would have to tell him the truth. And if it turned out to be the wrong thing to do — well, so be it. Any certainty would be an improvement on the continued half-truths that she was forced to tell. As she settled back in the battered seat, holding Jeremy's hand, she prayed fervently that her decision would be the right one, not only for Nick and herself but also for Timmy, who after all had more right than anyone to be considered in this tangled situation.

CHAPTER EIGHT

'Do you think he looks worse?' Rose murmured the words, leaning close to Nick, fearful that Jeremy's parents would hear what she was saying. Though with the constant background hum of the plane's engine, it was doubtful. But Ann Morgan seemed to have a sixth sense anyway where her son was concerned, and every move that Rose or Nick made in the care of their patient she watched with large shadowed eyes, as though trying to read their thoughts.

The drive to the airport had been accomplished without any hold-ups, and the taxi which brought the Morgans pulled up alongside the aircraft almost as soon as the ambulance itself had arrived. The loading on to the plane had been straightforward. Nick had simply lifted Jeremy in his arms and climbed smoothly up the few steps into the narrow body of the plane before laying the little boy gently on to the stretcher.

Since their departure, his condition hadn't altered at all, and he remained completely still, despite Rose's careful efforts at trying to stimulate some response.

With a reassuring smile towards the worried parents, Nick took the ophthalmoscope from his case and peered into first one of Jeremy's eyes, then the other. Apart from the noise of the engines, there was silence as Rose and the Morgans held their breath.

'I think there may be some rise in intra-cranial pressure, but it's difficult to be sure,' said Nick.

'We won't have to ventilate, then?'

'No, I think giving Jeremy oxygen via the face mask will be enough for now.' Nick bent forward and patted Ann's tightly clenched hand. 'There doesn't seem to be much change so far. But if your son should need help with his breathing, we might, just might, have to put a tube down and connect him to our ventilator.' There was a worried gasp from Jeremy's mother.

'Now hopefully it won't come to that,' Nick said quickly, 'but a very important part of the treatment for patients with head injuries is to give them lots of oxygen—what we call hyperventilate. It helps the swelling of the brain to settle and cuts some of the risk of damage caused by the rise of pressure inside the skull.' He picked up a small black box, like a radio, pulled a lead free from one side and clipped the end to Jeremy's forefinger.

'This is a pulse oximeter, and it measures the amount of oxygen in the blood.' There was a pause as they all waited for the figures to appear on the tiny screen. 'There you are!' Nick held the machine round so that the Morgans could see the numbers. 'Ninety-two per cent—that's an excellent reading, especially as we have a reduced air pressure in the aircraft. Nothing to worry about on that score at the moment.' He smiled reassuringly. 'I shouldn't think any of us have a better reading than that.'

'Would you be able to treat him while we're here in the plane if necessary?' Tony Morgan swallowed, his face pale under his tan.

'Oh, yes, we've got everything we need on board. But I don't know yet if we'll have to do it. I just wanted to warn you, because I didn't want you to think there was some panic if we go ahead.'

The poor things! Rose thought sympathetically. It must be agony for them to have to cope with this. I'd go mad if Timmy had anything wrong with him.

She scrambled from her seat. 'Shall I make some coffee? And if you're hungry, we have sandwiches.'

'I couldn't eat a thing, but I'd love a cup of coffee,' Mrs Morgan muttered quietly.

Rose edged carefully along the gangway and pulled out the cups and some packets of biscuits. By the time she had juggled the full cups of coffee back to the other three and made coffee for the two pilots, the lines of strain on the faces of Jeremy's parents seemed to have lightened, and Ann Morgan even managed the ghost of a smile as she nodded her thanks.

'Will Jeremy be able to remember the accident when he comes round?' Tony set his cup in one of the small holders by his seat and leant forward, his dark grey eyes fixed on Nick.

'It's difficult to say. The brain is an unknown quantity in many ways and doesn't always respond as we would expect it to. If and when Jeremy recovers, he obviously won't remember anything of the flight.' Nick stroked the little boy's fair hair back from his forehead. 'And it's very likely that he might not remember the accident at all.' He stared for a long moment without speaking, and Rose waited with trepidation. Was he thinking of his own loss of memory? She knew that he found it very frustrating, not being able to recall parts of his life.

'I know of a case,' Nick continued softly, 'a colleague who has lost part of his memory, and even several months later it still hasn't returned. Of course, emotion also plays a large part in loss of memory. Unpleasant happenings can be shut off by the brain.'

Rose stared as he continued speaking. Surely *his* experiences during their travels in East Africa hadn't been unpleasant enough to cause his mind to shut them away? She had been frightened, even terrified at times, but Nick had never shown the slightest hint during the whole of their journey of being anything other than completely in control.

Hastily she dragged her mind back to what he was saying.

'There is one very big advantage when children are injured. Even if part of the brain has been damaged, and we don't know for sure that it's the case with Jeremy, the brain is often able to develop new pathways, and so young people stand a much better chance of making a good recovery.'

'If anything happens to him. . .' Ann's words faded as she seized her son's hand, holding it against her cheek.

'Until we have the opportunity to do the full tests,

with a scanner and more X-rays, we can't tell you anything definite. But, as Jeremy hasn't really shown any signs of deteriorating so far, I'm cautiously optimistic, shall we say? And now if you'll excuse me, I'll try and catch up with the details we have.'

Nick picked up the file and began reading intently, and after a moment Rose collected the cups and put them tidily into a black rubbish sack, before returning to the rear seat of the plane. It was obvious that Nick didn't want to say too much more about Jeremy's condition. As he had told the Morgans, until they could get more investigations done, it was impossible to try and forecast the outcome.

She stared sympathetically as Ann hunched at the side of the stretcher, clutching Jeremy's hand as though the sheer force of her grasp could help him.

'How much of your holiday had you taken?' Rose smiled encouragingly at Tony. He seemed withdrawn, hardly looking up as she spoke, and she had to strain to hear his muttered words.

'We got to Corfu last week.'

'Was it your first visit?'

He shrugged his shoulders, not speaking, as he sat with his head hung forward, his hands loosely clasped and elbows resting on his knees.

'If you don't mind talking about it, it might help to know exactly what happened when Jeremy was knocked down.' In the pause that followed, as Tony obviously tried to gather his thoughts, Rose could feel someone staring and turned to look at Nick. Though he didn't say anything, she was conscious of his approval of her efforts at trying to distract the anxious father from his brooding.

Nick might not as yet remember their first meeting, but on occasions such as this there seemed to be an affinity between them that had been apparent from the moment they'd met.

A picture flashed into her mind, of how their thoughts had often travelled on the same lines when they were on their trek, and it was comforting to realise that such closeness was still there underneath the present strains. The smile that lit up her face, bringing a depth of colour to her eyes and a glow to her fair skin, brought an answering grin from Nick. His white teeth were a flash in his saturnine face, his eyes crinkled into a myriad finely webbed lines at the corners. Rose looked away hurriedly, afraid he might read from her expression just what his smile could do to her responsive heart.

Hastily she carried on her conversation, chatting to Jeremy's father, with an occasional interruption from Ann, and it didn't seem too long before the seatbelt lights appeared on the bulkhead and they were approaching the airport at Liverpool.

The landing on the well marked runway was as smooth as silk, and directly the aircraft swung to a halt, Nick had the door unlocked and the short flight of steps set down to the ground.

A smiling face greeted them as Rose and the Morgans started to clamber from the plane.

'All right, love?' Their ambulance was waiting, the driver reaching out a hand to help them alight, before his bulk moved lightly to the inside of the plane. He and Nick between them lifted the unconscious boy carefully from the stretcher into the waiting vehicle.

'Well, Timmy, I don't think your daddy can have forgiven me. After all, he hasn't been in touch since we got back from Liverpool.' Gently Rose swooped the gurgling baby from his warm bath and laid him face down on her lap, patting him dry and smoothing sweet-smelling talcum powder into the tiny creases of his body.

He stared back wide-eyed as she turned him to face her before laying him on the soft fluffy blanket on the bedroom floor. She always enjoyed his bathtime, and this evening it was more than usually comforting to her despondent spirits.

Since Alan and Marjorie's return from New York, she had only spoken to Nick on one occasion, and that had been during a chance meeting at the office.

She shivered as she remembered their quarrel. Its start had been so trivial, and as she now thought back to their return flight, once they had delivered Jeremy and his parents to the Liverpool hospital, she still had the same sensation of nausea that she had felt at the time. Perhaps she had over-reacted. Nick had merely tried to put his arm around her, and she had pushed him away, turning abruptly towards the window.

He had obviously been offended, and when Rose refused yet again to go out with him socially, his eyes had darkened in sudden anger. But she knew that if she dared to spend a relaxed evening in his company, she would find it well nigh impossible not to betray how she felt, and also the fact that he was Timmy's father.

'I don't have to ask why you won't go out with me.' Nick had muttered the words in her ear, causing a *frisson* of nervousness to prickle at her spine. 'I can see you still have feelings for Timmy's father, so why can't you be honest enough to admit it? You seem to delight in tantalising me at every turn, when you know how I feel towards you.' He had paused, his face white and angry, his mouth a narrow line as he'd seized her chin in one hand and forced her to look at him.

'Or perhaps you don't like the idea that I can't remember part of my life, that I'm some sort of mental cripple. You don't fancy the idea that I might have some unpleasant secret that I haven't told you about. Is that it?' He had sighed deeply. 'Well, every relationship must be dependent on trust, and as you either don't trust me or are hankering over your past, I think our relationship had better be strictly on a business footing from now on.'

Rose had been speechless, her idea of confessing everything to Nick shrivelled to nothing in the blast of his unexpected anger.

'I think you're mad,' Melanie had told her bluntly when she'd returned to the flat. 'I'd always baby-sit for you, you know that. What are you going to do, fence around with the poor guy until you drive him completely from you?'

'You don't understand,' Rose had sighed.

'No, I jolly well don't! He obviously cares for you.

You should just forget all your stupid hang-ups and try to start the relationship again from scratch.'

'That's what Nick wanted to do originally,' Rose had muttered.

'Well, there you are, then.' Melanie had left the kitchen with a toss of her head. It was the nearest the two friends had come to quarrelling in all the time they had known each other.

When Rose finally plucked up courage to ask Alan for news of Nick, the director merely said that Nick was busy on a project at one of the London hospitals and would no doubt be in touch once he got back.

I'm not too sure of that, thought Rose with a sigh as she picked up the white plastic bath, took it to the bathroom and emptied out the water, hurrying back to the bedroom to cast a wary eye on her son. Timmy seemed to be growing so quickly, and though still a week away from five months, was able to wriggle himself around in a manner that was enthralling but at the same time very nerve-racking for his anxious mother.

'Come on, little one, let's get supper organised. You can play in your chair.'

Firmly holding her son's wriggling legs, Rose tucked his clean white nappy into place before putting him into his high chair in the corner of the kitchen.

'No more teeth yet?' She peered intently into his gaping mouth. 'Just my luck that I missed seeing your first tooth immediately it appeared. No wonder Beverley was so eager to tell me about it, after we got back from Liverpool! You'd have thought she was the proud mother!' Smiling to herself at the memory of Beverley's excitement, Rose slipped her forefinger gently along the edge of Timmy's gum. No, nothing new since she'd last looked.

She moved to the sink by the window. The evening sun cast long shadows in through the back door and the scents from the garden blended with the aroma from the coffee-pot, bubbling attractively on the front of the stove.

'Melanie should be in soon, hope she's in the mood for salad, it's far too hot to attempt anything else this evening.'

She ran water into a bowl and dropped in two large potatoes, scrubbing half-heartedly and putting them into the microwave ready to switch on when Melanie got back. It only left the lettuce to wash; Rose perched on the edge of the stool and gazed into the tiny garden, thinking back again to her last meeting with Nick. He still showed no signs of regaining his memory, and she was beginning to wonder if all her fretting and soul-searching was doing her any good. Would he ever know exactly who she was?

'Hi—where are you?' Rose got slowly to her feet at the sound of the front door opening and Melanie's cheerful shout echoing from the hall. She picked Timmy from his chair and pushed on the switch of the microwave oven in passing, stopping abruptly in the doorway of the sitting-room as she saw the figure standing just behind her friend.

She stared at Nick, drinking in the sight of him. His dark hair was brushed back from his face, and dressed formally in a grey suit and white shirt he looked somehow unfamiliar. She was unaware of the picture she made herself, with Timmy resting easily on one hip. Her thick glossy hair was scraped into a blue ribbon which matched her full-skirted cotton dress. The weight she had lost during Nick's absence made her eyes look larger than ever. With a shrug, she walked into the room without speaking, her bare feet silent on the carpeted floor.

'I thought you were away in London,' she murmured uncertainly, scarcely noticing that Melanie had left them. Seeing him again, Rose realised just how low in spirits she had been while Nick was away.

Surely she wasn't starting to rely on his being around? The idea that she might be set her heart beating fast; anxious that he shouldn't read how she felt from the look on her face, she moved to the settee and saw awkwardly, bouncing Timmy gently on her knee and trying to ignore Nick's expression.

'I should have been in touch before,' he said softly, moving to the settee and sitting beside her. 'But after we got back from Liverpool, I wasn't sure if you'd want to see me again.' He took her hand in his and studied it intently, gently separating her fingers. 'I don't know why I was so angry. Put it down to the fact that I'm so often frustrated by not knowing everything that's happened to me. I may have told you before that any sort of mystery sets me on edge because of it.' He leant towards her, his face only inches from her own. 'And I sense a mystery about you, whenever I try to get to know you better.'

'There's no mystery about me,' Rose said firmly.

'Oh, no?' Nick bent towards her and looked deep into her eyes. 'What about a certain telephone call between yourself and Melanie?'

'I don't know what you're talking about.'

'Rose, I'm not trying to pry, but this does concern me, so I feel I have a right to ask you about it.' He paused, and Rose could feel her heart beating nervously.

'I was going through the tapes at the office with Alan, and on one of them there was a short section where you and Melanie were discussing arrangements to do with Timmy.'

'So?' Rose took a deep breath. Where was all this leading?

'You mentioned my name, so I have no doubt you meant me. Unless you have another friend called Nick?' He waited as Rose shook her head once more, then leant back against the big padded cushion. '"I don't know how much to tell Nick." Isn't that how it went?'

Suddenly Rose realised just what it was that Nick was talking about. 'Actually, it was a private conversation. . .' she began, but Nick rested one finger on her lips.

'Perhaps I shouldn't have listened,' he said softly, 'but if you have something to tell me, especially if it has any bearing on the time I lost my memory, won't you put me out of my misery?' Impatiently he waited for her to speak.

'I can't remember exactly what was said. No, please, let me finish.' Abruptly she pushed his hand away. 'I'm sorry, but whatever it was, I can't think of a thing that I can tell you...'

She flinched as the harsh sound of his laughter cut into her words, for there was little humour in the sound. 'This to-and-fro relationship reminds me of one of the mating dances in Africa, where the young women flaunt their attractions for the young men to view, but there's no question of them getting together before all sorts of rituals have been completed.'

'I don't flaunt my attractions,' Rose said huffily, edging away and placing Timmy on his blanket on the floor. Using the move as an excuse to stop the physical contact between herself and Nick, she sat cross-legged near the baby, pulling Timmy's toy box beside her and taking out his favourite plastic rattle.

'I didn't mean that exactly.' Nick sighed, running his hand through his hair and immediately looking more like the Nick she knew. The depth of his sigh was enough to cut her in two, and again she wondered if she should risk the truth, for it was obvious that his uncertainty was causing him a lot of heartache. She studied him as he took off his jacket, throwing it carelessly on to the chair, and undid the knot of his dark red silk tie.

'That's better. Now what were we saying?'

Rose shrugged, not looking at him, all attention apparently fixed on her small son.

'I...er... I...er....' But before she could gather her thoughts into some semblance of order, Melanie burst into the room.

'Sorry to interrupt. Are you eating with us, Nick? If so, I'll throw another potato into the microwave.'

'Not literally, I hope.' A mischievous grin lit his face as he looked towards the door and Melanie's blonde head. 'I haven't anything planned, and I'd be delighted to accept. If you're sure I won't be in the way?'

Saved again! Rose thought thankfully. But I can't put it off for much longer. It isn't fair to Nick, it isn't fair to me.

But her anxious musings were interrupted again, this time by Timmy's cry of protest as he rolled awkwardly off the edge of his rug. Before she could rescue him, Nick stretched forward and swooped the baby into his arms, and Timmy's cry settled into a gurgle of delight. He snuggled into the crook of Nick's arm, contentedly chewing at his thumb, his gaze fixed on the man who held him, an occasional gummy smile spread across his face as Nick muttered soothing noises in the baby's ear.

'Do you know,' Nick grinned after a moment, 'this son of yours really likes me. See how comfortable he is!'

'He's like his mother, goes for the dark, sinuous type,' giggled Melanie, pushing open the door and setting crockery and cloth on the battered dining-table in the corner.

'Melanie, that's not funny!' Rose muttered furiously, her colour spreading over her face and neck. Swiftly she jumped up from the floor and busied herself with the laying out of the dishes on the table. 'Anyway, I'm supposed to be doing that. You've been working all day.'

'Just sit down and chat to Nick. I'm fine,' Melanie said softly. 'You've got just about everything ready. There's only the lettuce to wash. Are cheese salad and jacket potatoes all right for you, Nick?' she called.

I wish I could be as relaxed with him as Melanie, thought Rose. She moved back across the room and watched Nick as he talked unselfconsciously to her son. It was true what he'd said—Timmy was comfortable with Nick. She could tell by the soft murmuring noises the baby made as though in answer to Nick's voice.

'Come and get it!' Before Rose had time to worry about Nick's reaction to Melanie's remark, the food was ready. Taking Timmy from Nick's arms, Rose sat the baby in his swing chair and stood back as Nick moved to the table. She wasn't sure whether she was glad or sorry that Melanie was with them. On the one hand, it postponed any chance of serious discussion between herself and Nick. On the other, the problem of Nick and his loss of memory wasn't going to go away, and she would have to do something about it before too much longer.

Melanie's carefree chatter as they sat at the table and began their meal certainly helped to smooth over any sticky patches in the conversation. Rose felt a sudden lightening of her spirits. Another reprieve from the worry of trying to decide what to do. She felt a moment's guilt at her cowardice, then mentally shrugged.

As she was lucky enough not to have to face her problems at the moment, she had every intention of enjoying her meal. She cut a crust from a slice of bread and placed it carefully into Timmy's grasp, then picked up her knife and fork.

'Could you pass the butter, please?' Smiling nonchalantly at Nick, Rose cut open her potato and watched with almost greedy delight as the golden butter melted into its hot white centre.

'Salad, anyone?'

CHAPTER NINE

IT WAS silly to feel so excited, but Rose couldn't stop the grin of delight that swept across her face. It was like being a child on Christmas Eve or the day before the start of the school holiday. With a sigh of anticipation, she leant forward in the seat and peered out through the tiny window of the plane. Below, like a thread of silver running through the desert, the Nile, exactly like a storybook illustration, lay beneath. A tiny shadow, no bigger than a pinprick, seemed to her excited stare to follow the route of the plane as they travelled further and further south.

'You look as though you're enjoying yourself.' Nick bent close, smiling indulgently.

'I am. How about you?'

'Well, I might not have the best sort of welcome when we get there.' He grimaced, the predatory line of his olive features sharpened into the likeness of an eagle, his nose and chin emphasised.

'What do you mean?' All her excitement dissolved in a moment as Rose stared back at him open-mouthed.

'I wouldn't win a popularity prize in some parts not a million miles from where we're going,' he explained.

'Yes, but. . .'

'Hey, don't get upset! I shall be sorry I mentioned it if it's going to spoil your pleasure in the trip.' He put an arm around her and hugged her close for a second, then got up from his seat and moved smoothly to the front of the tiny air ambulance, bending forward to speak to John, their pilot.

Rose stretched back and stared at the men in the front of the plane, studying them through half-closed eyes. She realised she had forgotten once again just how small the air ambulances were. Once the stretcher had been fitted, taking the place of three or four seats, there was barely room to struggle along the tiny gangway, and the tail of the aircraft seemed scarcely big enough to accommodate their equipment. She glanced over her shoulder at the selection of well-fitted cases, mentally listing everything on board. Ventilator, heart monitor, pumps to measure the giving of drugs, a selection of tubes and all that was needed to set up care for any emergency. In fact, it could easily be transformed into a miniature intensive care unit in the sky.

'How about coffee?' Nick turned towards her and mouthed the words, his voice inaudible above the constant background throb of the plane's engines. Rose nodded her thanks and picked up her novel, but the words on the page in front of her were far less interesting than her journey, and after a moment she placed her book on the floor and gazed once more from the window.

It wouldn't be long before they had to land again for refuelling, before going on to complete the flight to Mombasa.

Rose had had many doubts at first about leaving Timmy for three days to take on the job of picking up a patient in Kenya. But both Alan and Marjorie had persuaded her that the trip right away from everything might be what she needed. Once she had decided that it wouldn't do her son any harm to be without her and in Marjorie's care for such a short time she had happily made arrangements. Though she had been surprised at the wrench she'd felt as she delivered Timmy to Marjorie's capable hands the previous evening.

But then the fact that Nick had organised his work to act as the doctor for the trip had been completely unexpected, and rather spoilt the object of her trip—to get away and forget all her problems. He had obviously pulled strings to make sure that he went with her, and his pleasure at the arrangement had been apparent from the time they had met at Gatwick in the dawn light of a crisp morning. Presented with a *fait accompli*, Rose had given up on her worries. And gradually excitement had taken over.

'Here we are.' Balancing the cups on a small tray, Nick moved easily along the plane, then handed her the coffee before returning to the small hot-water boiler, neatly set in a cupboard just behind the pilots' seats. He was back almost immediately, with a tray of sandwiches and rolls, and the two of them sat side by side, enjoying a snack lunch in a companionable silence.

'Shouldn't be long before we get to Port Muran to refuel.' Nick spoke the words close to her ear, and his warm breath sent prickles down her spine. But she managed to nod in a nonchalant manner, still anxious that she shouldn't betray how much any physical contact with him could set her pulses racing.

'How long will we be on the ground?' she asked.

Nick shrugged.

'Not too long, I hope. It's not the most luxurious area in the world to hang about.'

'Not exactly wash-and-brush-up time, then,' Rose laughed, remembering some of Nick's vivid descriptions as they had flown south.

'Definitely not.' He patted her hand. 'Now I'm going to try and get some shut-eye. We never know when we'll get a chance to sleep on these longer trips, so I suggest you do the same.'

Without another word, he leant his head back against the seat and was soon breathing steadily, the corners of his mouth turned up in a half-smile, a lock of thick dark hair falling forward over his forehead and lending an air of unexpected vulnerability to his stern features.

Rose gazed at him intently, taking the opportunity to feast her eyes on his face, an opportunity she so seldom had. It still surprised her that he hadn't any suspicion so far about Timmy, had not as yet recognised his own features in the face of his son.

Since his meal at the flat the previous week, he had developed the habit of calling in, ostensibly on his way home, turning up regularly at bath and feed time.

Though Nick showed no sign of recognising any likeness, he had developed an obvious fondness for the baby, happy to play with him when he visited and never resentful that Rose appeared tied up with her duties as a mother. She couldn't help the way her thoughts had run on, savouring the idea of the family they could so easily be, watching them eagerly to see if the physical resemblance would betray her secret.

But so far there had been no sign of Nick's memory returning. She pushed aside the worry about the future. She didn't know what she would do if he never recovered it, but in the meantime he seemed happy to spend time with her and Timmy, and had shown an unexpected tenderness towards his son, that brought a lump to her throat when she thought about it.

'Fasten seatbelts.' Nick's voice cut into her reverie, as he snapped instantly awake with the lighting of the seatbelt sign.

'Wish I could do that,' muttered Rose, looking away hastily, afraid that her face might betray what she had been thinking.

'Do what?' Nick stared at her, puzzled.

'Wake up instantly. I always stumble around for about half an hour like a zombie when I first get up, completely unbearable to be with.'

'Remind me not to marry you, then.' He grinned, completely unaware of how the joking words sent tremors through her. But despite the way she felt, Rose managed to grin back as she clicked her belt into place and rested her head against the seat.

She turned and stared down at the approaching ground, a smile dancing about her lips as she pictured the two of them together with Timmy, imagining family scenes that brought a dreamy expression to her face. Timmy growing up with them both, becoming more and more like Nick, whose slow-burning smile and loose-limbed walk melted her heart every time she saw him.

But she paused, the unwelcome possibility bursting into her brain like a fire-cracker; if Nick never recovered his memory, such an idyllic situation would be impossible.

She glanced at him from the corner of her eye, as he studied the approaching airfield from the small port on his side of the aircraft.

'How long will we be here for refuelling?' she asked. But Nick obviously didn't hear her, for just at that moment the flaps, then the undercarriage snapped into place and they were skimming a dusty field that looked almost completely deserted as the plane juddered on the uneven surface of the ground. The narrow streak of tarmac was full of potholes, making the aircraft bounce like a ball as it touched down, despite the expertise of the pilot. Rose had flown with John several times in the past; he was the most senior and most experienced pilot in that company's fleet, so it said a lot for the poor condition of the surface that even he was unable to manage a smoother landing. The engines screamed into reverse thrust, stopping any attempt at conversation, before the plane swung at the end of the runway and taxied towards a small hut, from which several figures appeared, their white robes fluttering like flags in the breeze.

'Here we are.' John scrambled from his seat and moved to the door, pushing up the restraining bar, and flicking out the small flight of steps.

'Whew!' gasped Rose, as she followed Nick and caught the blast of the heat from the ground which shimmered in waves that made it difficult to see the surface properly. She stumbled at the bottom step and would have fallen if Nick hadn't swiftly caught her, holding her close for a long moment.

The strength in the slim lines of his body was deceptive, his muscles like whipcord as his arms encircled her waist. She felt completely safe with him, protected from any hazard that might arise; she made no attempt to break free, lost in sensations that she hadn't known since her previous visit to Africa.

'Are you all right?' He stood back and looked down at her, his expression unreadable behind his dark glasses.

Rose couldn't prevent a small intake of breath as she stared at him. Though his clothes were so different now, his crisp white shirt and lightweight trousers barely creased in spite of the journey, she had such a strong recall of their first meeting, it made her giddy. Almost as though he could remember as well, his hand smoothed gently at her hair, pushing it back from her face.

'Are you all right?' he murmured. 'You looked— I don't know, almost as though you were going to faint just then.'

Despite the furnace-like heat, Rose shivered.

'Just someone walking over my grave.' She

laughed nervously. She took off her sun-hat and fanned at her face. 'Is there anywhere we can sit, somewhere in the shade preferably, while we're waiting?'

She turned to John, busy working out fuel requirements as he talked animatedly to an official who looked cool and relaxed in a blue cotton suit. Rose couldn't help a smile at the sight of the official's pen, like some unicorn's horn, jutting out over his forehead, as it stayed tucked firmly in the thatch of his black curly hair.

'There is a waiting area of sorts. Come along, we'll rest there while the pilots deal with their business.' Nick took her arm and ushered her through an arched doorway in a sandstone building that blended almost completely with the surrounding landscape.

An overhead fan lazily shifted the hot air from one corner of the room to the other, bringing a not unpleasant smell of the plaster walls and ceiling to her nostrils. Even that small amount of movement gave an illusion of a cooler atmosphere than the temperature outside.

Rose sat down on a padded seat near the door as Nick went purposefully towards a young black girl who leaned on a chipped wooden table, her long striped cotton dress tight against one thrust-out hip.

Rose couldn't hear what was said. The heat seemed to have numbed her senses, and there were so many reminders of her previous visit to Africa that she had difficulty in deciding what was real now and what was memory. Even Nick's personality seemed to have changed from the considerate, almost gentle person she had become used to, and he now had an arrogant stance and more than ever resembled a hawk, his features sharpened dramatically.

There was a short gurgling laugh from the girl at the counter, accompanied by a swift grin on Nick's face, before he turned and walked back to Rose, two cola cans in his outstretched hand.

'I'm afraid these aren't chilled, but at least it's a drink while we're waiting.'

Rose nodded her thanks, puzzled that Nick should have bothered with drinks in the dusty untidy room, when they had a drawerful of cool cans in the plane. But she sipped the liquid gratefully, its fizziness tickling the back of her throat and bringing some refreshment to her dry mouth.

'In case you're wondering why I bought these drinks here,' Nick whispered, obviously reading Rose's thoughts, 'I wanted to have an idea of the political situation, to see if anything has changed since I was here last year.'

'And has it?' Rose frowned, wondering how on earth a young girl in a dusty provincial airfield would have any idea of what was happening.

'Most areas near where we're going are peaceful, though occasionally fighting with some of the rebels can and does break out in the more outlying parts of the border country,' he told her.

Rose pulled herself free from the padded seat, her cotton uniform trousers sticking uncomfortably to her legs as she moved.

'And what does that mean for you?' she asked.

'Well, we shouldn't have any problems collecting Mr Matteson from Mombasa.'

'I hope you don't mind me asking,' Rose sat down again as Nick perched on the seat beside her, 'but why on earth did you take the chance of coming on this trip when there's still some risk in it for you?'

'I have my reasons. They seemed to make sense to me when we organised the flight.' He swallowed from his can and then stared at her, a devil-may-care look to his eyes that made Rose's stomach contract painfully. 'Now I'm not so sure.'

'We're not in any real danger, are we?' Her heart started a rapid tattoo. She remembered how long it had taken her to recover before, how she would wince at a car backfire or the slightest crackle of thunder. She couldn't face the thought of any uncertainty on this trip. 'I'm not getting into a situation that might be dangerous,' she said sharply. 'I've got Timmy to think of, and if there are doubts, I demand we make arrangements to turn round right now.'

'Don't be stupid, Rose!' snapped Nick.

'I'm not being stupid—how dare you? My son needs me far more than the patient, and as I said, any hint of danger and I don't go on.'

Nick frowned, draining his can of drink, then crushing the tin into a small flat disc. 'Do you think that even if I'd been prepared to go into a dangerous situation, Alan would have agreed to your coming as well?' His expression was cold and the easy friendship that had existed between them disappeared in a way that churned at Rose's inside. But she had no intention of taking back her words. Timmy was and had to be her first consideration, he had no one else, and it was vital that she get back safe and sound. And not even the way she felt about Nick could change that fact.

For what seemed an age there was silence, broken only by the sound of her breathing as she struggled to control her rapidly rising temper. A soft flap-flap from the fan broke into her thoughts. Nick stared down at her, his look so evocative of the arrogant way he had behaved when they first met that Rose was almost smothered by well-remembered feelings and sensations.

Suddenly Nick shrugged his shoulders and grinned, his bad temper gone in a flash. He pulled her to him, planted a kiss on her forehead and tucked her arm beneath his own.

'I wouldn't let anything happen to you, so don't start to get so agitated! Let's see if they've finished refuelling the plane and we can get away to somewhere more comfortable.'

Only partly reassured, Rose allowed herself to be hustled into the outside glare, and was relieved to see that the tanker and the hand pump that was used to fill the plane had been packed away and the men in their long white robes were drifting from the runway and hovering in a line by a broken fence.

'Time to go, folks.' John beckoned them from the doorway of the plane, scrubbing at his hands with a tissue, to remove the last traces of fuel. 'I shan't be sorry to get airborne, either.' He wiped a hand across his forehead. 'The heat today seems unusually oppressive.'

Silently Rose climbed aboard the little aircraft and struggled past the stretcher to her seat at the rear. Absently she clipped her belt into place, then leaned back and closed her eyes. She needed time to think without interruption from Nick. Their relationship, which she had hoped was moving along in a pleasant fashion, even though it lacked the passion of their first encounter, was still vulnerable, and the idea was more upsetting than she would have thought possible.

For a moment she had almost hated Nick, when he seemed to think of danger ahead with excitement rather than the dread that she had experienced at his words.

She sighed deeply, as the engines roared into life and the little plane made its short run before lifting suddenly into the air.

Her high hopes of the trip looked as though they could turn out to be just wishful thinking. That Nick might remember something when they were in similar circumstances was obviously too much to hope for. She carefully opened one eye and peered at him. It was true, the feeling she'd noticed when they were having their drinks. He was almost fizzing with excitement, and she couldn't bear the idea that there was even a remote possibility that the horrors of that earlier trip, which now seemed a lifetime ago, could be repeated.

At least the flight progressed smoothly. They moved ever further and further south, the ground visible through thinning banks of cloud that drifted below them in gossamer trails. Rose stared down at the changing panorama underneath, watching as the dull sandy colour of the desert country gradually changed in texture to deep patches of green.

'We shouldn't be too much longer.' Nick, who had remained at the front of the aircraft during the flight, watching the pilots' instruments with absorbed interest, walked easily to Rose's seat at the back and stretched out beside her. His long legs in cool dark cotton trousers were dangerously near her own, and carefully Rose edged along the seat, smiling at the same time in an effort not to give offence.

Nick yawned, showing strong white teeth. 'God, I'm tired! On flights like these, you sometimes feel as though you're condemned to fly on into increasing darkness for ever and ever, like some modern-day Flying Dutchman.'

Rose stared from the window, surprised to see the gathering shadows of night drawing in around the tiny body of the plane. A sky of deepening blue velvet, sprinkled with diamond flashes of starlight, reached away to the horizon as the constant warning lights on the wings signalled their progress through the night sky.

'How much longer?' she queried, before turning to the window and studying their reflections in the darkness.

For a moment Nick didn't answer. She could see the outline of his face staring towards hers, and a flutter of nervousness stirred at her inside.

'I should think we'll be heading down towards

Mombasa very soon. We've just about cleared the Highlands and should soon be over the coast.' He leaned across her and peered from the window. 'Not that you can see anything very much now. I would imagine those lights could be Nairobi, but I'm not a hundred per cent sure.'

Rose held her breath. The feel of his body pressed against her own brought a surge of remembered sensation that she was finding hard to control.

Nick gazed into her face, his eyes only inches from her own.

'You're not frightened of this trip, are you?'

She shook her head, thankful that the sweep of her hair partly covered her face. Even though the aircraft lights were very dim, she could see the glitter in Nick's gaze as he studied her.

'I'm not nervous, just excited.' She cleared her throat. 'Does any of this help—you know, bring back any memory?'

'No, I don't think it's likely to. I think I have to accept that the part of my memory lost after the accident is gone for ever.'

He edged away from her and sat back, his hands clasped behind his head, his elbows resting against the back of the seat.

Rose settled herself primly, smoothing at the line of her uniform trousers, conscious of the scent of Nick's aftershave and the masculine essence that was such a strong part of her memory of him. Even during the difficulties of their trek, he had always smelt so clean, just as he did now. His scent, the way he moved, even the taste of his kisses, were printed forever on her mind; she knew she would be able to recognise him if she were blindfolded.

But no matter how vivid her recollection of their time together, it wasn't likely to be of any help to Nick.

He spoke again, almost dreamily. 'I sometimes wonder if I'll ever find someone who can fill in the missing bits for me.'

'Wasn't there anyone with you at the time who could tell you exactly what happened?' Rose held her breath as she waited for his answer. She felt that if she concentrated hard enough, perhaps the sheer force of her memories would bring back Nick's by some sort of osmosis.

'It was impossible to get a full story.' Nick reached forward and picked out a couple of cans from the drawer under the seat. He cracked one open and raised it in enquiry. Rose shook her head, waiting impatiently for him to continue.

'I'm sure it wasn't because the memories were unpleasant. Sometimes in my dreams I can remember sensations that were. . .' He paused and looked in her direction, a mischievous expression on his face. 'Well, I don't think I'll go into detail, if you don't mind.' He drank thirstily. 'I have a definite impression of something good, which in the circumstances isn't very likely. Are you sure you don't want a drink?'

'No, thank you. Just carry on talking,' she said softly. It was as though they were cocooned in unreality, the little plane holding them close in an unexpected intimacy, an intimacy she wanted to go on forever.

'I've said enough.' To her disappointment, Nick pulled out the medical folder, switched on his small overhead light and began studying the pages intently. The magic moment had passed, and they were back to their roles of doctor and nurse. Biting her lip, Rose picked up her own work sheet. She had to drag her mind away from Nick Coleman and the complications in her own life. Soon they would be landing, and her prime consideration then would be Mr Matteson. Mr Matteson who had fractured his pelvis and leg when a safari truck had tipped over on to him. Not only was there a possibility of a ruptured bladder, but it sounded from the details they'd been given that he might have developed an infection in a deep wound of the thigh. It wouldn't be an easy case for them to look after, and, if she could just push aside her own emotional problems, Rose knew she would enjoy the challenge.

CHAPTER TEN

'*JAMBO.*' The softly spoken Swahili word of greeting was as gentle as the dark night air around them. Sighing with fatigue, Rose lifted her medical case on to the Customs counter and rested her back wearily against a bar which separated them from the main concourse of the airport. All the pleasant, almost euphoric sensations of their journey had gone, lost in a fatigue so deep it seemed to smother her in velvet. She felt as though they'd been travelling for days, not hours, and now that they had finally landed at Mombasa, if she didn't soon lay her weary body on to some cool sheets, she knew she would expire!

After the comfortable temperature of the aircraft, the heat in the airport wrapped itself around her body like a warm damp blanket, and she scratched impatiently at the small rivulets of perspiration irritating the length of her spine.

Nick looked as cool and fresh as when they'd started out, his crisp white shirt a flattering contrast to his olive skin.

'How do you do it?' Rose muttered enviously as they waited for the paperwork to be completed.

'Do what?' Nick stared down at her.

'Manage to stay looking so cool. I feel as though I could melt! And when you think it's—what? Midnight, local time? Goodness knows what the temperature will be like in the morning!' She knew she sounded petulant, but try as she might she couldn't prevent a note of complaint from creeping into her voice.

'Hey!' Reaching towards her, Nick flung an arm around her shoulders and pulled her to him. 'Don't get all crabby, now. Everything has gone so well so far. I know you're tired, but we'll soon be at the hotel.' He leant closer and whispered the words in her ear. 'And it's fully air-conditioned. You won't have to worry about not being able to sleep because of the heat. And no mosquitoes either.'

'I'll still have to take my anti-malarial drugs, though, won't I?' Unable to stop herself, Rose leaned into the circle of his enclosing arm, enjoying his nearness and the way he made her feel so safe and cared for. At times like this it didn't seem possible that there was any distance between them, and she knew it would be so easy to tell him everything, and hang the consequences.

Surely knowing the truth would be better for Nick than having part of his life a blank? He was such a strong person in every way; and, getting to know him as she had over the past few weeks, Rose was sure that for him even the most unpleasant certainty would be preferable to not knowing.

Anyway — a smile touched her lips at the thought — there was nothing unpleasant about herself and Timmy, surely? He obviously cared for them both. He might well be delighted with his instant family, and he wasn't the sort of person to jib at his responsibilities.

She sighed. And that was one of the reasons she felt such doubt at telling him. She didn't want to be a 'responsibility', but rather the woman he loved and wanted to spend the rest of his life with.

'Penny for 'em.' Nick's voice made her blink as she realised that Nick, John and the co-pilot were all waiting, ready to leave the Customs area. She'd been so lost in her thoughts, it hadn't registered that their luggage had been cleared and their passports stamped.

'Sorry.' Embarrassed, she hurriedly picked up her case and walked with the three men towards the large open doorway that led to where their taxi was parked.

'Where were you just then?' laughed Nick. 'Obviously miles away. I thought for a moment you'd actually fallen asleep on your feet.'

'I am tired,' Rose admitted, 'and I was thinking. . .oh, well, it wasn't important.' Liar, she told herself sternly. But it wasn't something to be worried over now, especially as she was so tired. She could only hope that Nick's return to Africa would stir memories for him. He was obviously pleased to be back on the continent he loved so well, an air of excitement almost seeping from his skin as they climbed into the taxi.

Their flight had been one of the last to arrive, and the airport and surrounding area was deserted, with very few people around.

Rose couldn't prevent a shiver as she rested her head against the cracked leather of the taxi interior, the musty aroma making her nose twitch involuntarily.

She wasn't sure if it was just her tiredness, but a feeling of dread, like the dark tropical night which stretched around the little group, seemed to smother her earlier hopeful anticipation.

The taxi, a worn-out Cadillac, stuttered into life as their driver, looking over his shoulder at his passengers crowded into the rear, treated them to a smile as wide as a slice of watermelon, his teeth shining in the gloom of the vehicle.

They set off without speaking, apart from the occasional apology as the road surface, a series of bumps and hollows, jostled them together. Palm trees, occasional cedars and shrubs that hung low over the dusty footpaths appeared in the dull glow of the vehicle's lights. Rose saw one or two rundown-looking stores whose dimly lit interiors had a few shoppers even at this late hour. The only lights on the road came from petrol stations, harsh neon signs that lit up small patches of bare earth and more dusty palms, before the taxi plunged once more into the darkness of the African night.

Rose's relief at the sight of the hotel brought a gusty sigh to her lips. It was a delight, a myriad small bungalows set among sweet-scented bushes, the main reception area built of glass and polished wood; everywhere dark faces smiled in greeting, despite their late arrival.

'Would you like a drink?' John turned to them as they finished signing in at reception.

Rose ignored the look of appeal that crossed

Nick's face as she quickly shook her head and muttered, 'Goodnight.' She didn't understand why she should be feeling so downcast, but tiredness weighed at her legs like lead, every step an almost overwhelming effort as she followed the blue-jacketed figure of the bellboy to her own room.

'Thank you, thank you,' she murmured as he showed her where all the switches were situated, flung back the door leading to a cool tiled bathroom which seemed to be full of large fluffy towels and turned up the force of the air-conditioning as she asked.

'Goodnight,' he smiled, half bowing his way from the room.

Barely able to keep her eyes open long enough to take a shower, Rose fell thankfully into bed. A tray of fruit, bread and coffee on a low table in front of vividly striped curtains looked inviting, and she managed to summon enough energy to peel one paw-paw and savour the sweet juiciness before sleep claimed her.

The knocking at the bedroom door rattled into her dream, a dream where she was trying to encourage an older version of Timmy to call an impatient Nick 'Daddy'. The sight of Nick's face as she staggered sleepily to the door and opened it felt like a continuation of the dream. She couldn't prevent a gasp as for a moment she wondered if Nick could sense what she was thinking.

Then reality struggled into her sleep-sodden brain and she managed a smile at Nick's bright enquiring look as she tied the belt of her bathrobe more firmly.

'What time is it?' she yawned.

'Just after six.'

'What?'

'I wondered if you'd fancy a swim. It's the coolest part of the day, and we can't risk burning that tender skin of yours, now, can we? The hotel has a private beach area overlooking the Indian Ocean.' His enthusiasm made her smile, despite the fact that she had barely woken up. The resemblance between the man standing on the broad wooden step of her bungalow and the older version of her son in her dream was so strong that Rose had to struggle to stop herself giving Nick a hug. Especially dressed as he was in shorts, with his shirt completely undone, making him seem younger and more relaxed.

'I'd love it, but I haven't brought a swimsuit,' she said regretfully.

'No problem. There's a shop in the main foyer of the hotel. I'll get one for you.' He spun on his heel, then glanced over his shoulder. 'Size twelve all right? I'll be back in a few minutes.'

'Are John and Andrew coming as well?' Suddenly Rose wondered if an early swim alone with Nick was such a good idea.

But he ignored her words, moving down the curved brick path towards the main reception area, brushing against a brilliant scarlet-flowering shrub as he went and sending a drift of scent into the air.

Hastily closing the door, Rose switched on the tiny kettle and made herself coffee, gulping it down in hurried mouthfuls, her heart beating like a drum in anticipation. Looking from the broad French windows, she could just see a strip of sand and the pearly edge of the water. A faint trail of mist moved across it, giving the scene a dreamlike quality.

By the time she had drunk her coffee, put a call through to Alan and Marjorie and hastily showered and cleaned her teeth, Nick had returned.

'I'm sorry,' he grinned mischievously, 'but I could only get this one in your size.'

He delved into the bright blue carrier bag and produced two minute scraps of sea-green material.

'I can't wear that!' Blushing in horror, Rose stared at the diminutive bikini.

'Well, I suppose we could always go skinny-dipping. I'm game if you are.'

'Don't be silly!' Flustered by his teasing, Rose snatched the swimsuit. 'Wait there. If it doesn't fit properly, you can forget the swim,' she snapped, closing the door firmly in Nick's face.

She had to admit, despite its brevity, the swimsuit fitted perfectly and flattered her figure. Her breasts, though fuller since Timmy's birth, were still firm, her stomach and hips as trim as before. As she stretched the scrap of material across her bosom and stepped into the cutaway briefs, Rose felt a stirring of devilment.

Perhaps if he saw her in this state of near-undress, it might jog Nick's memory as her sober uniform hadn't done. Retrieving the white bathrobe from the bed, she wrapped it round her and stepped on to the front step of her bungalow, looking shyly at Nick from under her eyelashes.

'There are to be no sexist remarks,' she said

sternly as Nick guided her towards the beach and the soft sounds of the ocean.

'Cross my heart,' he laughed. 'In fact, if it would make you feel better, I won't even look at you until you're in the water.'

Rose sniffed deeply at the fresh morning air. Perfume reached her nostrils from the multi-coloured bushes that stood in clumps in the hotel garden. To her enchanted gaze it was like a brand-new world, everything sharply defined in the crystal air. They saw no one else, and Rose couldn't prevent a sigh of pleasure as they walked in the shadows of the palm trees to reach the sugar-white sand, delighting in the feel of it between her toes. The mist had risen above the surface of the sea, revealing its blue-green depths.

'We're lucky the hotel is on this part of the coast.' Nick paused as they reached the edge of the sand. 'Further north, the water's very shallow and there's quite a stretch of mud before you get to it.'

'I don't want to know about anywhere else.' Rose tossed her head. 'I can't imagine anything more beautiful than this.' She swept her arm in a huge circle and began spinning faster and faster on the spot until she fell full-length in a laughing heap.

Laughing with her, Nick pulled her to her feet. 'Come on, time for our swim. As I promised, no peeping. See, my eyes are firmly shut and I'll keep them like that until you're submerged.'

Rose stared suspiciously as he waited for her to take off her bathrobe and dive into the inviting ripples of the Indian Ocean. His lean muscular body was as powerful as she remembered. There was no shyness in the way he stood, his brief multi-coloured shorts emphasising the long lean thighs, his shoulders trim yet beautifully proportioned.

But she couldn't prevent a gasp as he ostentatiously turned away, when she saw the scar that rippled with the movement of his body and formed a curved cicatrice across his back. He had been much more seriously injured than she'd realised. She gave an involuntary shudder at the thought — he could so easily have been killed. With a determined frown, Rose made up her mind. There would be no more shilly-shallying from her, for Nick had been brought back to her life, and there had to be a good reason for it. Fate, whatever, had given them another chance, and she was going to make good use of it. At the first opportunity, she would tell him the whole story and accept the consequences.

'What's the matter?' Obviously wondering at her long silence, Nick turned and stared at her; there was a pause, as he looked up and down the length of her body, his eyes appearing smoky in the increasing sunlight.

'You promised you wouldn't look!' Rose squealed as she snatched up the discarded robe and held it in front of her.

'I didn't intend to.' Nick's voice was husky. 'But when you gasped just then, I thought something was wrong.' He moved slowly towards her, his feet stirring the sand into ripples of movement. 'Come on, mermaid, let's have our swim, shall we? If I continue to. . .' He broke off and with a sudden change of mood took the robe from her, seized her hand and, ignoring her cry of protest, pulled her into the water.

'It's so warm!' Subconsciously prepared for the chilly waters at home, Rose was surprised by the sensation as the silky depths moved around her. Surfacing, she pushed her hair back from her face and turned away from the beach, not stopping to look at Nick's powerful body, which followed just behind her, his effortless crawl scarcely disturbing the surface of the sea.

'Race you!' He moved up close, drops of water clinging to his lashes, his eyes as dark as night and as difficult to read.

'Where to?' asked Rose, looking round for some point to land.

'The small landing-stage over there.'

She wasn't sure how she would cope with getting out of the water under Nick's admiring gaze, but she set off with a will and was pleased that she kept up very well, reaching the small wooden platform only seconds behind him.

'Up you get!' Easily, he swung his body over the edge of the stage and turned, reaching down into the water to take her hand.

'I'm quite happy where I am.' Pushing her hair back again, Rose paddled energetically, resting one arm on the edge of the platform, trying to appear at ease. But in reality her heart was beating fast with nervousness at the way Nick's eyes narrowed as he stared down at her.

'Come on, don't be silly,' he repeated a shade

impatiently. 'I'm not going to make personal remarks about your figure, I promise you.' Before she could protest again, he swung her easily on to the raft beside him and then lay back without a glance in her direction, closing his eyes against the sun, which was rising rapidly, deepening the colour of the sky to a cornflower blue.

'This feels good.' Rose stretched out beside Nick. The wood was warm and comfortable on her back, and she gave herself up to the pure sensual enjoyment of the moment, the taste of salt on her lips, the feel of the water as the drops clung to her limbs, the scent of the clean salty air. In such perfect surroundings, all problems melted away. Perhaps now would be a good time to tell Nick the truth.

'It's like heaven, isn't it?' she murmured softly, not sure if he heard her words as she pondered aloud. 'It only needs one more thing to make it perfect.'

'Oh, and what's that?' Before she could gather herself together, Nick turned on to his stomach and peered close into her eyes.

'Having Timmy here, of course,' she said nervously, aware of the lines of his body so close to her own, the length of his powerful legs, his thighs touching hers and causing a myriad prickles to cascade over the surface of her skin.

'Rose, Rose,' Nick murmured huskily. 'Can't you forget Timmy for a minute and concentrate on me?' Lazily he traced the line of her cheek with his forefinger, trailing it gently across her mouth. 'You're putting all sorts of wicked thoughts into my mind!' He kissed her softly. 'Perhaps we shouldn't have had this swim,' he whispered. 'It could have unlooked-for results.'

'How can I forget Timmy?' Rose began, but her words were abruptly halted as Nick's mobile mouth pressed on to hers with a kiss that gradually drove the breath from her body. For a moment she lay unresponsive, conscious only of the taste of his mouth on hers, the slight saltiness from the seawater, the tang of his sun-warmed skin filling her nostrils.

Slowly the pressure of his kiss deepened, and despite her efforts at self-control, Rose's arms moved with a life of their own, her fingers touching the springy tendrils of his hair, softened now after his swim, as they clung in the nape of his neck. The firm control she had maintained till now when in Nick's company slipped away, her mouth opening under the pressure of his, her body moulding into him. Gently her fingers traced the scar that travelled down the curve of his chest, sliding in the dampness of his sea-soaked skin.

'Oh, Rose,' Nick murmured huskily, 'this feels so right. Don't try to fight me now, don't hold back. I can tell that you feel as I do, as though we'd known each other for a long time.'

Rose barely heard his murmuring voice. Was this why he'd asked her to go for a swim? Had he planned something like this when they reached the raft? If it was, she didn't care, reckless abandon seizing her in its grip. Her whole body was a mass of sensation, sharp yet sweet. She was immersed in the taste, the scent, the feel of the man who had filled her thoughts and longings for so many weeks, ever since his devastating return into her life.

She was suddenly aware that Nick had pulled away, his breathing ragged in his throat. He raised himself on one elbow and stared at her, his eyes half-closed in passion, the sensual lines of his mouth curved upward in admiration as he softly slipped the strap of her bikini top down over one smooth shoulder.

Suddenly another sound broke into her thoughts, jolting her into an awareness of her surroundings; the putter-putter of a small engine. A voice hallooed near at hand, and with a muttered curse Nick sat up as Rose, her heart beating fast, seized the wispy bikini top and covered herself. Her hands trembled so much with the emotions Nick's lovemaking had stirred in her that at first she couldn't get the strap to sit straight.

Ignoring the two dark-skinned boatmen who grinned across at them from a small outrigger, Nick helped her to pull her swimsuit into line, then turned towards the men, baring his teeth in a travesty of his usual grin.

'*Jambo*!' he called, waving one hand in salute.

'*Jambo*. Do you wish to return to the shore?' The younger one was frankly curious as he stood easily on the swaying craft, one hand gripping a central upright pole. The older man kept his eyes downcast, though he had been the one to call a greeting.

Breathing hard, his nostrils white with tension,

Nick shook his head, and with another wave they steered with a single oar as the boat drifted away.

Not attempting to say a word, Rose dived into the water and struck out for the shore.

'Rose, wait!' But she ignored Nick's call. If the fisherman hadn't called out to them just at that moment, she would have given in to Nick's lovemaking, and just suppose she'd become pregnant again? Her life was in enough of a turmoil without having to cope with another baby. But oh, how she had wanted him, and even as she waded from the water's edge and on to the now burning hot sand, her whole body seemed to be melting with the longing that Nick's caresses had aroused in her. In the welcome shade of the palms, she turned and stared towards the raft. Nick was still sprawled out, his arm resting across his face, looking completely at ease.

'All right for him,' she muttered moodily as she walked quickly to her bungalow. 'He obviously doesn't care that we were seen in such a compromising situation.'

Her thoughts raced on. She would make sure that she kept well away from any fishermen or outrigger boats during the rest of her stay in Mombasa.

'There definitely isn't an ambulance available, is that what you're saying?' Nick moved the telephone receiver to his other hand and shrugged his shoulders as Rose looked at him questioningly. 'When could we have the use of one?'

She sat back in the large leather chair in the main foyer of the hotel and stared towards the door. Since breakfast, Nick had been on the phone almost continuously. What should have been an easy journey to fetch their injured patient was held up by one problem after another.

She pricked up her ears as he began speaking again. In one way, it was a relief that there had been so much to arrange, for it had stopped any chance of personal confrontation between herself and Nick. She had hurried to the dining-room once she had showered and dressed after her swim, thankful to be able to share a table with their two pilots.

The food and service were superb, in keeping with everything else in the hotel, but Rose found her appetite gone. Her few feeble efforts at conversation with John and Andrew faded as soon as they began. She barely nibbled at some fruit and hot rolls, but drank cup after cup of the excellent coffee in an effort to assuage a thirst that scorched at her throat. As soon as Nick arrived, she had excused herself from the table, waiting in her room until he'd called her from the reception area. Now she sat on the edge of the large comfortable chair, poised as though for flight, dreading any discussion with Nick about what had taken place.

'There's only one ambulance that's suitably fitted out to carry someone as severely injured as Mr Matteson, from what I can gather.' Nick pushed his hand impatiently through his hair and flung himself into the seat beside Rose. 'It's no more than I might have expected, because though the medical service does very well with what's available, when all is said and done it's still a poor country.'

'What do we do now?' At first Rose felt a flicker of apprehension that Nick was about to refer to their lovemaking out at the raft. Every time he opened his mouth to speak, a flutter of nervousness caught at her insides, for she didn't know what her reaction would be if he mentioned it.

But he seemed to have put the episode completely from his mind, treating her in such a cool, professional manner that she began to wonder if she'd dreamt everything that had taken place. But no, it had been all too real. She ran an exploratory tongue across her lips, recalling vividly the taste and feel of Nick's mouth on hers, then she realised that, lost in her thoughts, she had missed part of what Nick was saying.

'. . .taken Mr Matteson to a safari lodge not too far from where he had his accident, and there's a doctor there, so at least he isn't languishing in the bush,' Nick explained. He looked as assured as ever; even his bush shirt and trousers fitted as though made to measure. Rose had to stifle a surge of memory, seeing him in such similar clothes to the first time they had met; it brought a tumble of thoughts to her mind that stirred such longing that she felt sure Nick would be able to guess something of what she was thinking.

'I think we'd better have a word with John, find out what arrangements he's made about the plane, then get hold of a safari Land Rover and drive to where Mr Matteson is staying.' Talking half to himself, Nick hurried back to the desk, and soon he and Rose were side by side in a vehicle which was painted in dazzling zebra stripes along one side. But despite its bright appearance it still seemed to find every pothole in the road they drove along. Very soon they were covered in a thin film of dust, as on their first trip, and the sight of a group of gaily dressed children who waved merrily from the kerbside transported Rose back once more.

'How long will it take to get there?' She barely glanced at the shabby buildings and mud-track road as they came to the outskirts of the town. If the similarities of their present journey didn't jog Nick's memory, she was determined to explain everything to him. And travelling together now might be her last opportunity to say something.

'Are you all right?' Nick's voice was low and she had to strain to hear what he was saying.

'I'm fine,' she said bravely, wondering if he was going to bring up the subject of their swim.

'I don't feel I owe you an apology for this morning, but if I caused you any offence. . .' He stopped speaking as they came to an even more bumpy piece of track, struggling with the steering-wheel as the truck jounced and threw them about on their seats.

'There is something that I learned this morning.' As the road levelled out again, Nick smiled wickedly, turning to look at Rose for a brief moment before he faced the front once more.

'And what was that?' Despite her efforts at coolness, she couldn't prevent a tremor creeping into her voice.

'You want me as much as I want you. If you do still feel anything for Timmy's father, it hasn't stopped you—how shall I put this?—it hasn't made you unresponsive to others.' He laughed softly. 'In fact, I had a definite impression at the time that no one could have been further from your thoughts than Timmy's father.'

'How dare you, you arrogant. . .!' Rose was unable to continue, almost struck dumb with temper at Nick's clinical assessment.

'Honey, don't get mad,' he drawled.

'Don't get mad?' she echoed. 'Why did you suggest the swim?'

'I wanted to prove something to myself, something I've suspected for quite a while.'

'Ooh,' Rose gasped, 'the nerve of it! To take me out to that raft just to prove a point! Well, I hope you've come to a satisfactory conclusion in your little experiment. You always were an arrogant. . .' She stopped abruptly, aware of possibly saying too much, then recklessness took over. Why shouldn't she tell him?

But Nick had stopped listening. He seized her arm in a grip that almost took her breath away.

'Shh, keep quiet! Look over there.' Slowly he drew up, carefully pulling on the handbrake.

'What is it?' Rose whispered.

'Just behind that thornbush, can you see it? Merging with the patch of long grass.'

Rose peered intently, all thoughts of their quarrel forgotten. Suddenly she caught a glimpse of a tawny body, stretching lazily, a large head visible as the big cat yawned.

'Is it safe?' she asked nervously. The lioness looked awfully close to where they were sitting.

Nick leaned across the cab and took her hand. He seemed to have forgotten their fury of a few minutes before. A look of devilment crossed his face as he rested his lips in her palm, closing her fingers gently over the imprint of his kiss. Rose sighed.

'You have nothing to fear,' Nick murmured softly. 'Whatever you may think of me for my remarks just now, I would never let anything harm you. You have my word on that.'

Rose gave another sigh, this time of relief, as the lioness settled once more into sleep. Nick restarted the engine, his lips pursed in a tuneless whistle, the corners of his eyes crinkled against the glare of the sun as they continued on their route, on a track that ran straight ahead over flat grassland that stretched as far as the eye could see.

CHAPTER ELEVEN

CAREFULLY, Rose wiped Nick's face, but almost before she had finished, perspiration was running down on to the pillow, marking it with a patchy shadow that looked grey in the dim light of the room. In the two days since she and Nick had arrived at the safari lodge, he seemed to have lost so much weight, every bone stood out in sharp relief. What on earth was wrong with him?

Dr Rajan, the softly spoken Indian doctor who took care of the visitors and staff at the lodge, had said it definitely wasn't a malarial infection, though the shivering had looked to Rose like descriptions she had read of the illness. Obviously he would know more than she did about tropical diseases, but whatever it was, it was terrifying to see someone become so ill so quickly.

There was a soft tap at the door and Dr Rajan appeared in answer to her call to come in.

'How is Dr Coleman?' He moved silently to the bedside, his white cotton shirt and trousers a patch of lightness in the shaded room.

'He's still having the severe sweating attacks and doesn't seem to know where he is.' Rose could hear the tremble in her voice, but was powerless to prevent it. She had never felt so helpless in her life. Even when she had discovered she was pregnant and had heard the news, as she thought, of Nick's death, distance had helped to keep her feelings on some sort of even keel. But now, seeing Nick in his present state and unable to do anything for him apart from the most basic nursing measures brought her at times almost to screaming point.

'I feel I'm neglecting Mr Matteson. . .' Her voice trailed away. Though weighed down by the responsibility for their patient, she couldn't bear to leave Nick's bedside.

Thank heavens for Dr Rajan, she thought, taking a wet sponge from the bowl of iced water on the bedside table and once more wiping Nick's face.

He had been his usual self on their journey to the lodge. Following their brief argument, they had not mentioned their time on the raft again, and gradually Rose had lost her feelings of resentment and hurt. Soon she was thoroughly enjoying the drive over the grassy plains.

'Just think, people pay a fortune for the chance of a trip like this, and we're able to count it as work,' she'd said, thrilled at the sight of yet another pride of lions, and a glimpse of a stately giraffe as it swayed past, shyly trying to hide its dappled body and elongated neck behind a glossy-leaved tree.

Nick had smiled indulgently at her excitement, but she could sense that he was as thrilled as she was, particularly at being back in his beloved East Africa. Apart from once complaining of a headache, he had given no hint that anything was wrong.

The safari lodge, a single-storey building surrounded by a shaded veranda, had resembled a

Twenties film set, all sandalwood luxury and smiling staff in crisp white uniforms, whose greetings of '*Jambo*' had met them at every turn.

And, to the relief of both Nick and herself, Mr Matteson had been better than they had hoped, the antibiotics obviously helping to kill off the infection that had been such a problem.

Worn out by all the travelling, Rose had been deeply asleep when the knock had come at her door in the early hours of the morning. At first she had thought that the softly spoken servant was talking about Mr Matteson. But, as she scrambled out of bed and padded on bare feet in answer to the call, she was horrified when he had paused outside Nick's door and pointed inside.

It had only taken a moment's observation to see that Nick was seriously ill.

'Do you think we should try and get him back to England?' Now Rose watched nervously as the doctor completed his examination.

'I think we should first decide what it is troubling him,' Dr Rajan replied in his gentle sing-song voice. Everything about him was gentle, but at the same time he gave Rose a feeling of confidence that was the only good thing about her present nightmare. 'I have taken some blood samples and sent them to Nairobi. We were lucky: a supplies plane landed yesterday and we should have the results very soon.'

'If a supplies plane could land here, we could get the air ambulance to come and collect both patients,' Rose said eagerly.

'I do not think that would be wise, until we have

more definite information regarding Dr Coleman's fever.' Dr Rajan's face was sympathetic, but though he spoke quietly his manner was firm.

Rose sank back on to the chair beside the bed, dejection written in every line of her body. 'Why do you think he has such a high temperature?' she asked. 'It's been above forty degrees all day.'

'It may be partly a result of the high ambient temperature, of course. I will ask for another fan to be brought, and if you continue with the cool sponging I think that will do as much to help as any attempts at more formal treatment. You are right to be concerned, for it is not good for the brain to have to cope with such high temperatures.'

'The worst part is, he doesn't know me.' Rose lifted her hair from the back of her neck. It seemed unbearably heavy in the heat and, though she had tied it back when she dressed, tendrils had slipped free from the clip that held it in place and it hung in wisps, sticking to her skin.

'Even when his eyes are open, he doesn't focus properly,' she continued.

Dr Rajan patted her arm. 'That is certainly as a result of the fever.'

'You don't think it's a form of encephalitis, do you?'

'Inflammation of the brain? I think not. There have been no fits or anything of that nature.'

'Thank goodness!' Rose stared once more at Nick's face. His eyes were still closed, his cheekbones coloured by vivid flags of colour, the lines of

his face more than ever pronounced since the onset
of his illness.

'I will arrange for someone to sit with Dr Coleman
and give you a short break,' said Dr Rajan.

'I don't need. . .' Rose began.

'Nonsense, of course you do. You have had no
rest from early morning and you have only recently
had a long flight to get here. It would be very
unfortunate if you too were to be ill.'

Not waiting for her to agree, Dr Rajan slipped
quietly from the room, and shortly afterwards a
pretty African girl, in a white uniform dress, her
wide smiling mouth emphasised by her bright pink
lipstick, appeared and sat at the bedside.

'I'm Vanessa. I am to stay while you have some
rest,' she said softly, and after a moment Rose
accepted that she was very tired. And it was true,
there was no point in her driving herself so hard that
she became ill. Not that she had any intention of
spending too long away from Nick, but a light meal
and perhaps a swim in the Club pool would refresh
her enough to carry on with her vigil.

She walked slowly back to her room, her eyes
dazzled by the brightness of the afternoon sun. She
hadn't realised it was so late in the day. Time had
been an uncertain quality while she had been with
Nick, the minutes creeping past so slowly as he
showed no sign of improvement, and yet now it was
nearly evening, the day gone by without her
noticing.

She sank thankfully on to the cool cotton sheets
in her room, sniffing at a faint scent of something

like linseed, which blended with a spicy perfume from a purple-flowering bush outside the window. Though the room was plainly furnished, plenty of attention had been given to comfort. Some of the old furniture was old-fashioned, possibly from the Twenties, but there was a quiet harmony about the dark polished wood and the clean gaily coloured cotton bedcover and curtains. Kicking off her sandals, Rose stretched out on the bed, picked up the telephone and gave the number of the Fleetline office in answer to the receptionist's enquiry. With British time being two hours behind local, she had a very good chance of finding Alan on duty.

For a second she couldn't speak, unshed tears filling her throat as Alan's soft West Country voice sounded as clearly as if he were in the next room.

'What's the problem, love? I've had just a brief report from John. He said that Nick isn't very well, but couldn't give me any details.'

Rose sniffed hard. 'We got here the day before yesterday.'

'Yes, I'd worked that out. And what happened then?'

'They called me in the early hours of this morning to say that Nick wasn't very well. Oh, Alan, he has a terrible fever, is unconscious, and the doctor here doesn't know what it is!'

'Steady on! Nick's as tough as they come. Had he been complaining of feeling unwell?'

'No, that's what made it worse, somehow,' said Rose. He had a slight headache on the journey here, but nothing else at all. We'd just about got the arrangements sorted out for Mr Matteson. Nick thought he ought to have another day's antibiotic cover before we left, that's why we delayed our return.'

'Yes, he rang to explain that to me,' said Alan.

'Then this fever developed out of the blue, and he looks dreadfully ill.'

'It's not malaria, then?'

'No, according to the doctor here, who seems very on the ball. Not encephalitis, not dengue fever. His joints would be swollen with that, wouldn't they? Dr Rajan has taken blood samples and sent them to Nairobi, so I suppose we'll have to wait till the results of those come through, before we'll know any more.'

Already Rose was feeling calmer. Being able to discuss her worries with Alan, though he couldn't actually do anything, made her load seem lighter.

'Well, as your doctor said, until you see the results of the blood test, there's not a lot more to be done,' said Alan. 'I've arranged for the air ambulance to stay another day or so, but if it goes on any longer than that we'll have to think again. They were able to fit in a charter to take a businessman back to India who needed to get there in a hurry, so the insurance company hasn't started fretting about the delay as yet.'

'That's good. Now, on to pleasanter things — how's Timmy?' Firmly Rose pushed her worries about Nick to one side.

'He's a perfect baby, but you're going to hate Marjorie and me,' Alan told her.

'Why, what have you done?'

'We've done nothing, but I'm afraid another tooth has appeared.'

'Oh, the little perisher! Every time he produces a tooth, I'm not there with him,' groaned Rose. 'I reckon he does it on purpose.'

'Joking aside, he's fine, so you don't have to add him to your present worries,' said Alan.

'I don't half miss him! Give him a big hug and kiss for me, won't you? Anyway, I'd better ring off. This call must be costing a fortune!'

'Try not to get too despondent,' said Alan. 'If Nick can survive a mortar attack and goodness knows how long in a war-stricken area, I'm damn sure a bit of fever isn't going to. . .' The line faded in a series of crackling noises, and after shouting a hurried, 'Goodbye,' Rose replaced the receiver. Slowly she stripped off her T-shirt and khaki shorts, thankful for the cool drift of air on her skin as she went into the old-fashioned bathroom. With its temperamental water supply and a large white bath on curved legs, it reminded her of the ones in the nurses' home at her hospital training school. But the tepid shower was refreshing, and she stood under the water for several minutes.

Alan's remarks were very true. Nick was tough, a fighter. He hadn't survived all sorts of dangers just to succumb now to some sneaky illness. With a wry smile, she dried herself with a large fluffy white towel and pulled on the tiny bikini, her whole body stirred into memory by the feel of the material against her skin.

'Stop it!' she told herself sharply. '"That way madness lies".' Taking a striped robe from the bathroom door, she grabbed her towel and hurried along the veranda to the pool, a blue glistening patch among the glossy-leaved wild fig trees and acacia bushes.

To her relief it was deserted, and she slid gratefully into the water. It was much colder than she expected, and she shivered for a moment, before striking out overarm in a fierce crawl that rapidly ate up lengths of the pool.

She wasn't sure if it was a good thing or a bad thing that the lodge was nearly empty of guests. Apart from an elderly German couple who spoke very little English and honeymooners who kept themselves to themselves, Rose hadn't seen anyone other than staff since she and Nick had arrived. There was supposed to be a group coming later that evening, and she hoped fervently that there would be some younger members in the party. At a time like this, it would be pleasant to have someone to chat to and perhaps take her mind off her worries.

But at least the swim had given her an appetite, and as she towelled herself dry, for the first time that day she found she was looking forward to her meal.

Dr Rajan's advice had been sound, for she was feeling better as she returned to her room and changed into a bright turquoise sun-dress, carefully applying some eye-shadow and lipstick in an added effort to lift her spirits.

'He is still the same.' The nurse looked up reassuringly from her magazine as Rose poked her head around the door of Nick's room and stared at the outline on the bed. With a smile of thanks, Rose made her way to the small dining-salon.

'Good evening.' The two Germans nodded, their fine blond hair and pale skin flushed by the sun, making them look more like brother and sister than husband and wife. The greeting seemed to be the sum total of their English, for after that they ignored her, concentrating on their food as it arrived and saying very little even to each other.

There's nothing lonelier than eating on your own, Rose thought, as she studied the menu intently. I wish I'd brought a book to read, though I doubt if I could have concentrated on it.

The sudden tropical night had fallen, the lights from the veranda making the vegetation of the garden look almost black. The tapping of insects against the window screens, attracted by the red-shaded table lamps, provided a noisy accompaniment to the occasional clink of cutlery and rattle of dishes.

'I'll have a steak, salad and sweet potatoes, please.' Rose folded the menu and placed it face down on the table.

'Yes, Miss Maslen.' The waiter grinned with a flash of snowy white teeth. 'Anything to drink?'

'Why not?' Rose couldn't prevent a smile in answer to the man's infectious grin. 'A half-bottle of claret, if you have it.'

That should just about complete my relaxation programme, she thought, as she studied the ruby lights in the depths of her glass; though I must make sure I don't fall asleep at my post.

The steak was disappointing, being overcooked and stringy, but Rose was hungry enough to enjoy it anyway, and the various fruits that completed her meal — paw-paw, mangoes and a ripe pineapple — more than compensated.

'I'll have coffee later, if I may.' Rose put the napkin beside her empty plate and got up from the table, nodding her thanks in answer to the waiter's enquiry.

Neither one of the German couple looked towards her as she left the dining-room, and for a moment she was overwhelmed by a surge of loneliness that made her shiver despite the heat of the night. Exotic travel was all very well, she thought, if you were able to enjoy it, but she couldn't wait to see the runway at Gatwick lining up under the wheels of the air ambulance when they eventually headed home. In the meantime, there was Nick to take care of, and with a fast-beating heart Rose hurried to his room.

'He is fine, sleeping well. Dr Rajan was here a few minutes ago, and he will come in later to check that everything is all right.' With a squeak of her white rubber-soled shoes, the African girl left the room.

Rose threw her bag on the small bedside table and took hold of Nick's hand. His skin felt cooler to her touch, and when she bent to study him more closely his face in the lamplight was almost its normal colour.

But there was still no response as she softly called his name, and with a sigh she sat in the chair just vacated by her relief and leaned her head against the padded leatherette back.

God, but she was tired! The day had been endless, a constant worry since her early morning call when she had first been told of Nick's illness. She shook herself and picked up the magazine left by Vanessa and slowly turned the pages. But the words were a blur, and the soft background hum of the electric fan and the sound of Nick's steady breathing made her eyelids heavier and heavier. She kicked off her shoes, pulled her feet up under her and, clasping Nick's hand, soon drifted into a light doze.

'I've told you before, you should never go barefoot because of the risk of snakes.' Rose stirred, half asleep, anxious not to lose the pleasant dream that had made her smile. In her dream, she and Nick had been strolling through a patch of long grass, the stalks dried into an even beige colour, and suddenly Nick had swooped her into his arms and she'd realised that she was only wearing the tiny bikini.

With a start, her head jerked forward and she stared round the room, wondering for a moment where she was. She peered at her watch; eleven o'clock! She'd slept for three hours! Anxiously she looked at Nick, resting her hands on the edge of the bed, the dream still vivid in her mind.

There was the voice again, a trifle husky but the words plain.

'I've told you before, you shouldn't be sitting

there with your shoes off. God, I'm thirsty—any chance of a drink?'

'Nick? Nick?' Rose stared in wonderment. 'Do you know where you are?'

'Of course I know where I am. In Kenya.' His shadowed eyes looked steadily round the dimly lit room. 'How did we get to be in such luxury?'

'Don't you remember?'

'Of course I remember, Desert Rose. The truck broke down and I've been carrying Jacinta for miles. No wonder I feel so tired!'

'What did you call me?' whispered Rose. Had he said 'Desert Rose'? That had been his name for her during their original trek. He struggled up against the pillows, a frown digging lines into his forehead.

'Desert Rose. Hey, just a minute, something else. . . What are you crying for?' With every word his voice became stronger.

'I'm not crying,' Rose sniffed indignantly.

'Don't talk such rubbish, woman!' He lay back with a groan. 'I have the most terrible headache and I feel decidedly muzzy. If you love me, give me something to drink and then explain what's been going on.'

Brushing at her face with the back of her hand, Rose leapt to her feet and hurried to the door.

'I said you were crying,' Nick said softly. 'Where are you going now?'

'I'm going to call Dr Rajan. Oh, Nick, you've given us a terrible fright!' She broke off, not daring to say any more, and dashed from the room.

There was an impatient roar from behind her, but

Rose didn't stop to hear what was being said. She wasn't sure where Dr Rajan would be if he wasn't in the medical office, but her worry was unfounded, for when she got to the end of the narrow hallway that led to reception, she could see a sliver of light under his door.

'That is good news.' Dr Rajan got to his feet and followed Rose to their patient's bedside.

'How are you feeling, sir?' Reaching out a slim brown hand, he laid it gently on Nick's forehead, ignoring Nick's spluttering protests.

'I'm fine. I want something to drink, and this stupid girl. . .'

'Hush! She is not a stupid girl, she is a devoted nurse. Now, please be quiet while I finish the examination.'

Rose could scarcely believe her eyes or ears. Was this the man who earlier had been semi-conscious and burning with fever? In spite of Dr Rajan's request, Nick spent the whole ten minutes of the examination fidgeting and asking for a drink. His olive skin was still marked with a hectic patch of colour on each prominent cheekbone, but other than that he looked almost his normal self.

'Nick, for goodness' sake!' Rose protested, for every attempt by Dr Rajan to listen with the stethoscope or to examine Nick's eyes through the ophthalmoscope brought more annoyed comment from Nick.

'Well, I can't give you a diagnosis, but I can only suggest some sort of unusual fever, perhaps a virulent type of flu, who knows? We may have some better idea from the results of the blood tests.' Dr Rajan shrugged as he folded his stethoscope and put it in his pocket. 'However, it is obvious that whatever it was has more or less gone, so I think a few sips of water would be in order, and you must still continue with complete rest for a few days.'

'For heaven's sake, I can't hang around here!' snapped Nick. 'I've a patient to get away.' He threw back his head on to the pillow, unable to stifle an involuntary groan. 'But I must admit I've got a splitting headache.'

'Nick, it's all right. Mr Matteson is doing very well. You don't have to worry about him at the moment. Just do as Dr Rajan asks and you'll be better all the sooner.' Carefully Rose measured a small amount of iced water from the thermos into a glass and passed it to him. He drained it with one swallow, then stared at the two of them, confusion all over his face.

'Did you say Mr Matteson? What happened to Jacinta? I thought we were supposed. . . Hang on a moment, I've. . .' He lay back again, his frown deepening by the second. 'Who are you?' He pointed a finger towards Dr Rajan who himself, by this time, looked almost as bewildered as Nick.

'I think it's probably a good idea if I explain a few things. Dr Rajan, would you mind?' With a beseeching look, Rose gestured towards the door.

'Of course not. Call me if you want some help. I shall be in my office for at least another half an hour. Give Dr Coleman more drinks, for he must be very dehydrated after his fever,' he muttered quietly, as he slipped from the room.

Rose turned to Nick. He lay back on the pillow with his eyes closed, his powerful chest naked above the edge of the sheet. Not looking at her, he slowly beckoned, then held out his hand as she moved to the bedside.

'Do you want another drink?' she asked.

'Of course I do — I told you, I'm desperately thirsty. But even more than a drink, I want to know what's going on. My mind is such a hotch-potch, I can't make head nor tail of any of my thoughts.' Abruptly Nick flicked open his eyes and reached for her hand. 'First of all, where the devil are we?'

'I think I'd better begin at the beginning,' Rose said hesitantly.

'OK, but I want everything — and I mean everything — explained in detail. I'll have another glass of water first, because I think I'm in for a few shocks, judging by your expression. Put your shoes on!' he roared so suddenly, Rose nearly jumped out of her skin.

'You might be better as far as your illness is concerned, but you don't seem to have lost your. . .' she began.

Nick's grip tightened. 'Stop lecturing me, Desert Rose,' he pleaded. 'Just tell me the whole story.'

'Right, where is he? Where's my son?' Rose felt as though she was in the path of a whirlwind as Nick burst through the doorway of the flat and into the living-room, clutching the largest teddy bear she'd ever seen. Throwing it to one side, he lifted the baby from the carrycot, holding him at arm's length as he studied the tiny features. For a long moment Timmy returned his stare, his big dark eyes intently focused on the man inches from his gaze. Then, deciding he liked what he saw, Timmy stretched a chubby hand in Nick's direction before squealing in frustration as Nick still held him in the air.

Rose gazed longingly at Nick. It was the first time she'd seen him since his return. His jacket was snug on his shoulders, and she was relieved to see that he'd already put on most of the weight lost during his illness. His dark hair, cut much shorter now, showed the shape of his head, a shape that was at once strong yet aristocratic.

She watched the two of them, not trusting herself to speak. She still felt dazed by the speed of events that had occurred during the past two weeks. The hardest part had been leaving Nick in Kenya while she escorted Mr Matteson back to Britain, but she had agreed wholeheartedly when Dr Rajan had insisted that Nick needed more rest before flying home. In spite of Nick's fierce insistence that he was perfectly fit to travel.

If leaving Nick had been hard, explaining to him that night exactly what had happened had been even more difficult. His memory of his previous time in Africa was still patchy, the two visits melded into a confused whole, so that Rose found she had to repeat parts of the story several times before he would believe her. But though he remembered knowing her previously to joining Fleetline, she thought she'd brought on a relapse at his stunned silence when she had explained about Timmy.

'A son! I've got a son?' he murmured in wonder. At first Rose could have sworn there had been a suspicion of moisture in his eyes, but he quickly recovered, insisting yet again that he was more than fit enough to travel, especially knowing what he now knew.

'I can't really explain it,' Dr Rajan had said, when Rose had discussed with him Nick's partial return of memory. 'Possibly the very high body temperatures had an effect on the brain in such a way as to stir some memory into life. Who knows?' He had leant forward and patted her arm. 'But whatever the reason, it is good to know that Dr Coleman, even if he doesn't remember perfectly, recalls the most important part.' To Rose's surprise, he had winked extravagantly before turning back to his files.

'Hey, how about some coffee?' Abruptly brought back to the present by Nick's request, Rose hurried to the kitchen and filled the kettle, putting mugs on to a tray and getting Timmy's feeding cup with milk from the fridge.

The sun shone intermittently through the kitchen window, hidden at times by patchy cloud, and already the leaves were changing to autumn russet and gold. Rose had been waiting anxiously for Nick to contact her on his return, wondering the whole time what his reaction would be once he had had time to fully understand the implications of her news.

It was all very well for him to be so excited about

his son, but he hadn't yet been in touch with her to talk things over. Perhaps it was still too soon for him to reach any decision, perhaps he'd called round now to discuss their relationship further. Rose had to admit to feeling apprehensive as she spooned coffee into the mugs, poured on the boiling water and carried the tray back to the living-room. Supposing he didn't think there was any future for them?

She paused in the doorway, a lump in her throat. Nick hadn't heard her come in and was seated on the settee with Timmy on his knee. He was speaking so quietly, at first she didn't really hear what was said. But then the sense of Nick's words struck at her, and she hurriedly put down the tray, for she was having difficulty in holding it steady.

'As soon as your mother gets back with the coffee, I'm going to ask her an important question, and I want you to back me up.'

Rose wasn't aware of the small sound that escaped from her throat, but it was enough to attract Nick's attention instantly.

He laid Timmy gently in his carrycot and jumped to his feet. Taking Rose by the hand, he led her to the settee, then flung himself next to her, his arm stretched along the back, half turning so that his face was only inches from her own.

'What about the coffee?' protested Rose.

'Never mind the coffee for a moment. I have to talk to you.'

'But you just asked me to get. . .'

'Shhh!' Nick said sharply. 'You're making me nervous!'

'*I'm* making *you* nervous!'

'Rose, please listen, for goodness' sake!' His expression was serious, a small frown creasing his forehead.

'Rose, will you marry me?' The words shot from him with machine-gun rapidity.

'Nick, I. . .' Rose began. She had to grip her hands tightly together to stop them shaking.

Softly Nick laid a finger against her mouth.

'I think I can guess what you're trying to say. You're wondering if I'm asking you to marry me because of Timmy—am I right?'

'Not exactly.' Rose swallowed nervously. 'I was about to say that you mustn't feel you *have* to marry me because of him.'

'Rose, do you really understand me so little?' Suddenly Nick's lips were on hers, his hands moving through the heavy tumble of her hair, his body moulding her to him.

'Rose, oh, Rose, my love,' he whispered huskily. Softly his mouth trailed down the length of her face and caressed the pulse in her throat. 'I know I'm thrilled about Timmy,' he murmured against her skin, sending little shivers of delight through her. 'But I want to marry you because I love you, not because of some quixotic sense of responsibility. I've gone crazy at times over the past few months, thinking you loved someone else, holding back when I thought that another man had a greater claim.'

He sat back and stared at her, his dark eyes glittering with the force of his emotion. 'Don't you see? This is Christmas and birthdays all rolled into one, to have both you and Timmy.'

Dazed, Rose stared back, pulling her tracksuit top into line.

'I haven't said yet that I'll marry you.'

'Don't joke, Rose, I can't. . .'

Fiercely Rose put her arms around him and hugged him to her, her grey eyes sparkling with happiness. 'Of course I'll marry you, you idiot! I've loved you since. . .oh, since I don't know when.' Gently she smoothed his cheek.

'That's all I wanted to hear, Desert Rose, all I wanted to hear.' And once again he kissed her, his embrace full of the promise she'd waited so long to hear.

PENNY JORDAN

A COLLECTION

Volume 2

From the bestselling author of *Power Play*, *The Hidden Years* and *Lingering Shadows* comes a second collection of three sensuous love stories, beautifully presented in one special volume.

Featuring:

FIRE WITH FIRE
CAPABLE OF FEELING
SUBSTITUTE LOVER

Available from May 1993   Priced: £4.99

W RLDWIDE

Available from Boots, Martins, John Menzies, W.H. Smith, most supermarkets and other paperback stockists.
Also available from Mills & Boon Reader Service, Freepost, P.O. Box 236, Thornton Road, Croydon, Surrey CR9 9EL
(UK Postage & Packing Free)

SPRING IS IN THE AIR...

AND SO IS ROMANCE

Springtime Romance – A collection of stories from four popular Mills & Boon authors, which we know you will enjoy this Springtime.

GENTLE SAVAGE	– Helen Brooks
SNOWDROPS FOR A BRIDE	– Grace Green
POSEIDON'S DAUGHTER	– Jessica Hart
EXTREME PROVOCATION	– Sarah Holland

Available April 1993   Price £6.80

Available from Boots, Martins, John Menzies, W.H. Smith, most supermarkets and other paperback stockists.
Also available from Mills & Boon Reader Service, Freepost, P.O. Box 236, Thornton Road, Croydon, Surrey CR9 9EL (UK Postage & Packing free)

4 MEDICAL ROMANCES AND 2 FREE GIFTS

FROM MILLS & BOON

Capture all the drama and emotion of a hectic medical world when you accept 4 Medical Romances PLUS a cuddly teddy bear and a mystery gift - absolutely FREE and without obligation. And, if you choose, go on to enjoy 4 exciting Medical Romances every month for only £1.70 each! Be sure to return the coupon below today to: **Mills & Boon Reader Service, FREEPOST, PO Box 236, Croydon, Surrey CR9 9EL.**

NO STAMP REQUIRED

YES! Please rush me 4 FREE Medical Romances and 2 FREE gifts! Please also reserve me a Reader Service subscription, which means I can look forward to receiving 4 brand new Medical Romances for only £6.80 every month, postage and packing FREE. If I choose not to subscribe, I shall write to you within 10 days and still keep my FREE books and gifts. I may cancel or suspend my subscription at any time. I am over 18 years.
Please write in BLOCK CAPITALS.

Ms/Mrs/Miss/Mr _____ **EP53D**

Address _____

_____

Postcode _____ Signature _____

Offer closes 31st July 1993. The right is reserved to refuse an application and change the terms of this offer. One application per household. Overseas readers please write for details. Southern Africa write to B.S.I. Ltd., Box 41654, Craighall, Transvaal 2024. You may be mailed with offers from other reputable companies as a result of this application. Please tick box if you would prefer not to receive such offers ☐

—MEDICAL ROMANCE—

The books for enjoyment this month are:

LOVE BLOOMS Christine Adams
HIGHLAND FLING Margaret Barker
A CASE OF MAKE-BELIEVE Laura MacDonald
THE RELUCTANT HEART Elisabeth Scott

♥ ♥ ♥ ♥ ♥

Treats in store!

Watch next month for the following absorbing stories:

THE CONSTANT HEART Judith Ansell
JOEL'S WAY Abigail Gordon
PRIDE'S FALL Flora Sinclair
ONLY THE LONELY Judith Worthy

Available from Boots, Martins, John Menzies, W.H. Smith, most supermarkets and other paperback stockists.

Also available from Mills & Boon Reader Service, Freepost, P.O. Box 236, Thornton Road, Croydon, Surrey CR9 9EL.

Readers in South Africa - write to:
Book Services International Ltd, P.O. Box 41654, Craighall, Transvaal 2024.